THE MOONLIT DOOR

THE MOONLIT DOOR

A Nick Lawrence Mystery

Deryn Lake

This first world edition published 2014
in Great Britain and 2015 in the USA by
SEVERN HOUSE PUBLISHERS LTD of
19 Cedar Road, Sutton, Surrey, England, SM2 5DA.
Trade paperback edition first published in Great Britain and
the USA 2015 by SEVERN HOUSE PUBLISHERS LTD.

British Library Cataloguing in Publication Data

Lake, Deryn author.
  The moonlit door.
  1. Lawrence, Nick (Fictitious character)–Fiction.
  2. Vicars, Parochial–England–Sussex–Fiction.
  3. Murder–Investigation–Fiction. 4. Renaissance fairs–
  Fiction. 5. Detective and mystery stories.
  I. Title
  823.9'2-dc23

ISBN-13: 978-0-7278-8437-4 (cased)
ISBN-13: 978-1-84751-563-6 (trade paper)
ISBN-13: 978-1-78010-611-3 (e-book)

Typeset by Palimpsest Book Production Ltd.,
Falkirk, Stirlingshire, Scotland.

This book is in memory of three very dear people who all died within the same dreadful fortnight. Freddie Hodgson, wit, sophisticate, brilliant writer and friend; Jane Ray, one of the most beautiful women I have ever known, whose goodness to me was immeasurable; and Jackie Sellick, a kind, sweet woman from the old village days, who tied the most splendid bows I have ever seen. None of them will ever be forgotten.

ACKNOWLEDGEMENTS

My thanks and love are due to my third grandson, Fintan (Fin) Carroll, who sat with me on a sunny day in the garden and worked out the entire plot of *The Moonlit Door* (originally called *Mr Grimm's Men*). His notes were with me throughout the entire writing process. Thanks, too, to grandsons one and two, Henry and Elliot, who cheerfully turn up and with one swift movement put right whatever is going wrong with my mad computer. And last, but by no means least, my only granddaughter, Amelia, who does exactly the same but twice as fast.

ONE

I t was an ancient and attractive custom, one enjoyed by music-lovers and the stout-hearted but detested by those who were trying to get 'a decent night's kip', as Jack Boggis, the local misery, put it. The Vicar of Lakehurst, representative of the Church of England in a quaint and sometimes malicious village set in the heart of rural Sussex, had thought of restoring the tradition, and had been getting mixed reactions ever since.

It was all about a celebration of May. In years gone by, on May morning the choir had climbed up to the top of the church tower and raised their voices in song as dawn had lightened the skies. *Now is the month of Maying, When merry lads are playing Fa la la la,* et cetera. In fact, the lyrics were full of double entendres and rudery, much loved in the sixteenth century and ever afterwards. The original had been composed by Thomas Morley in 1595 and was the most famous of the English balletts – or madrigals. But despite the fact that it was all about sex, it was sung with much sincerity by as august a body as the choir of Magdalen College in Oxford from the roof of the Great Tower. But in Lakehurst people were not so keen.

'Can't get a wink of sleep after six,' Jack Boggis had proclaimed in the Great House, banging his pint of beer down on the table to emphasize his words. 'All that caterwauling from the church. Why can't they just sing at services like they used to?'

'It's a celebration of May, Jack.'

'Sounds like a lot of socialist nonsense to me. They'll be rolling tanks down the High Street next and we'll all have to cheer the Great Leader.'

He had expected a laugh but instead was met with a somewhat stony silence. The major, a relative newcomer to the village, having bought a house just outside with rolling countryside for a view, some three years earlier, cleared his throat and shuffled his newspaper. His wife, an attractive woman in midlife, concentrated fiercely on doing a crossword with an irritable little twitch of her head. Jack guffawed.

'I say that May Day was invented by the left-wingers. Whoever heard of it before Stalin?'

The major put down his paper and gave Jack a steely look.

'I hate to correct you, old boy, but it is a celebration as old as time. It's all to do with fertility rights. That song you object to so violently actually refers to it. The line about "barley break" is the ancient equivalent of a roll in the hay.'

Jack stared. 'Do you mean that the vicar allows them to sing filth from the church tower?'

'That filth, as you call it, is sung by children in Salt Lake City.'

'Well, they're American,' Jack retorted, and raised his newspaper.

Melissa Wyatt, the major's wife, kicked her husband gently under the table.

'What an old bore,' she whispered. The major merely smiled and nodded. 'Anything interesting in the paper?' she asked at conversational level.

'Not much. Another soldier killed in Afghanistan. Somebody or other punched someone else in the Big Brother House. Usual stuff. How's your drink? I'm going to have another.'

'I'll just go to the garden and check that Belle isn't making a nuisance of herself, then yes, please.'

She stood up and her husband saw her go out by a side door. When she had gone he sighed a little and picked up his paper but the gesture was rather to hide his face than to read. Much as he loved his granddaughter, Isabelle, he could not help but wonder that just as he had retired from the army and bought a new home in Lakehurst, there should have been that dreadful accident. An accident involving an articulated lorry and three other cars on that horrible A21.

That his son Michael should have been wiped out, that his pretty wife Chloe should have died a few hours later, was almost too much to bear. But it was the miraculous escape of their infant daughter that had altered Major Hugh Wyatt's life for ever. For from that moment he and Melissa had had to face the responsibilities of parenthood once more. Not that they would have done

anything differently, of course. But it was just that they had
reached the stage in their lives when things should have been
calmer, when they could have enjoyed their new home in
Lakehurst in peace and tranquillity. Yet it was not to be. Their
only other son, Ralph, was newly married and was moving from
place to place, a soldier like his father. There was nobody to take
on the responsibility of Isabelle but her grandparents.

Standing on the steps looking down into the Great House's
garden, Melissa smiled just a fraction sadly. Below her she
could see Belle playing on the swings, yellow bunches flying
as she called out, 'Push me harder. Push me harder.' Her play-
mate, another ten-year-old called Debbie, was valiantly trying
to obey but struggling somewhat. They both looked up as
Melissa called out, 'Are you all right, darling? Can I get you
another Coke?'

'Yes, please, Mummy. And some crisps.'

Melissa sighed inwardly. Crisps were not allowed so close to
Sunday lunch and she knew that Belle would squeal in protest.
But looking at the primrose head she felt a surge of protective
love, and weakened.

'All right, darling. But just this once. And you're not to eat
them all. Share them with Debbie.'

'Yes, Mummy.'

And Belle looked away and continued to swing.

Melissa went back inside to find her husband in conversation
with the vicar of Lakehurst, a delightful young man, in Melissa's
opinion, who never tried to ram religion down people's throats
but somehow by his very charm managed to involve them in
church activities.

'Hello, Mrs Wyatt,' he said, and shook hands enthusiastically.

Melissa smiled and transformed herself momentarily into the
beauty she had once been. A rather hawk-like face was softened
by the large blue eyes and the gentle curve of her lips. She looked
pretty and worldly simultaneously.

'Hello, Mr Lawrence,' she answered formally.

'I do wish you'd call me Nick,' said the vicar. 'After all, you've
been in the village three years now.'

'Is it really that long? I still feel like a newcomer.'

Nick grinned over his glass. 'So do I.'

'Surely not.'

'It's a tradition with the older generation. They think of you as a foreigner unless you've been born here.'

'Well, I'm afraid the foreigners are growing in number,' put in the major. 'The place is turning into part of the commuter belt.'

'Hear, hear!' came from behind Boggis's newspaper.

'Look who's talking,' whispered Melissa. 'You can tell by his accent that he's pure Yorkshire.'

Nick peered into the depths of his glass, his eyes catching something of the light thrown by the beer. Then he winked, a look which slightly disturbed Melissa.

'He's been in this pub so long he thinks he owns it,' he murmured.

Hugh Wyatt looked shocked and amused.

'That was a very unvicarish thing to say, if I may make so bold.'

Nick laughed. 'I quite agree,' he said.

He was an intriguing young man, Melissa thought, aged about thirty, with a squarish face and a lock of tawny hair that fell forward when he was talking seriously, somehow ruining the effect of his words. His eyes were clear and had a tendency to change colour slightly. His lips, though hardly virginal, had yet to find the impact of true love. He looked likeable, which, indeed, he was. Melissa smiled, enjoying his company.

Her husband, Hugh, was very much like the new generation of retired majors; keen-eyed, tight-jawed and various other clichés that suited his type. But behind that facade there was an intelligence and a quick wit. Melissa had fallen for those together with his charismatic smile and general charm.

He stood up. 'I'll just go and check Belle,' he said.

Watching him go out, bearing a bottle of Coke and a packet of crisps, Melissa gave a half smile. The vicar, somewhat to her surprise, caught her mood.

'It must be a great responsibility for you, bringing up a grandchild.'

She turned to look at him. 'Yes, it is. Of course, we wouldn't be without her. I mean, it is enormous fun having her around. It is just that . . .'

'Bringing up any child must mean a certain sacrifice of freedom.'

'We were looking forward to a bit of peace after army life.' Melissa shot Nick a quick glance. 'No, that sounds awful. I didn't mean it like that. Isabelle has brought us both a great deal of joy.'

The vicar smiled. 'I'm sure she has. She wouldn't like to come along to Sunday school by any chance?'

Melissa smiled. 'I can ask her.'

He grinned, and Melissa wondered why he wasn't married. Why somebody hadn't snapped him up years ago.

Hugh returned. 'Couldn't find the little wretch anywhere.'

Melissa looked alarmed. 'Is she missing?'

'No, I located her in the end. She was hiding in the bushes with Debbie.'

'Where was Johnnie?'

'Oh, he'd run off somewhere or other.'

'How like a man.'

'Now, now.'

Nick stood up. 'Well, I must be off. It's been so nice chatting to you.'

'Going to put your feet up?' asked Hugh.

'No, I've got to drive out to Fulke Castle and see Sir Rufus Beaudegrave.'

'Lucky old you. Mixing with the A-list, eh? I took Belle to the castle on a visit. She was very taken with the weapons they had on display.'

'Typical,' Nick answered. 'No, this isn't a social call. Sir Rufus has offered us a field when Lakehurst puts on its annual fête. I'm just going to finalize the details.'

'Is this the medieval thing I read about in the parish news?'

'Yes, that's the one,' the vicar answered cheerily as he made for the door.

'Waste of bloody parish money,' came from behind Boggis's copy of the *Sunday Telegraph*. 'Lot of people running about in fancy dress. Who do they think they are?'

'Perhaps they are enjoying themselves,' Nick muttered as he made his way out.

*   *   *

Despite his early start on the church tower, lustily singing 'Now is the Month of Maying', followed by Sunday communion, May Day falling on a Sunday, Nick felt in a buoyant mood and set off for Fulke Castle still humming the tune aloud. The fact that eighteen months ago there had been a murder there, a rather ghastly one – that is, if the taking of someone's life maliciously by another could be considered anything other than horrible – it failed to subdue Nick's sunshine mood. Fulke Castle had seen many deaths within its walls during its nine hundred plus years and therefore nobody considered the addition of one more as anything particularly significant.

As he drove along, Nick considered the extraordinary four years since he had been granted the parish of Lakehurst. Despite the grim times that he and the rest of the population had been subjected to – and some of the times had indeed been particularly unpleasant – he had fallen in love with the village, with its fair share of eccentric inhabitants, with the local people, even with the resident grumblers. Thinking of them as a multitude, Nick thought that they represented the whole human race in miniature.

The drive to Fulke Castle always inspired him by its beauty. Everywhere the countryside had burst into life with the spell of sunshine which had bathed it recently. Unlike last May 1st, Nick considered, when the choir had huddled in raincoats, grey-faced beneath umbrellas, while the lantern-jawed choirmaster had braved the downpour in a slouch hat from which a drip of water had descended at regular intervals. It had been a ghastly experience, particularly as Mrs Ely, amply built, had slipped on the descent and twisted her ankle. But today was different. The sun god in all its glory glittered high in the heavens and all was well with the world below.

Crossing the moat, Nick pulled up in the small car park and observed the castle for a moment before getting out. It rose in dramatic beauty, its other self reflected in the water that lapped at its feet. Like all buildings of a great age, various owners had added wings in their own particular style. Nick looked at medieval battlements, a Tudor dining hall – currently full of people moving slowly around with headsets on – delicate Georgian rooms, also lively, and finally the solid grandeur of the Victorian wing, where the family dwelt and which was not open to visitors. Getting out of the car and breathing in the fresh air, Nick made his way to the somewhat unimposing black front door which stood hidden round one of the corners. It was opened with a burst of laughter, and Nick smiled at Ekaterina, Sir Rufus's mistress, who had to all intents and purposes taken up residence with him. Officially she lived in London but she only went to her flat in Chelsea when she visited the theatre or went shopping. She was the incredibly wealthy and beautiful – but also, as it happened, incredibly nice as well – daughter of a late Russian oligarch.

'Come in, come in, my dear Nicholas. I spied you through the peephole.' And she indicated a Victorian copy of an arrow slit in the wall above. 'Rufus is doing his duty with the visitors – he does so occasionally. What can I get you to drink?'

'A very small and very weak tonic and gin. I'm serious. I've just had a pint in the Great House.'

She ushered him into the sitting room, a lovely place, Nick thought, with the Victorian heaviness gone, the only allusion to it being a chaise longue and a large plant in a burnished copper pot. Welcoming armchairs stood on either side of the fireplace, which today was covered by a William Morris inspired screen, while huge windows stretched down to the level of the moat itself, their shutters drawn back and partially hidden by floor-length red curtains.

'Take a seat, Nick, do,' Ekaterina said, her Russian accent quite pronounced, as always. 'Rufus will not be long.'

From the depths of an armchair as comfortable as it looked, Nick gave her an appraising glance. She had always been beautiful, gloriously so, but now she had an inner glow, a radiance that spoke of her being greatly loved by more than just a man, by children who also adored her.

It was out of Nick's mouth before he had had time to think of what he was saying. 'Are you going to marry him?'

A naughty little smile hovered round her mouth. 'How did you guess?'

'Well it wasn't hard.'

'We are getting married next month in London, at Chelsea Register Office. Then we are going to the Seychelles on honeymoon. Then we come home and want you to bless our marriage here, in the chapel in the castle. It will be my first proper wedding. I married my late husband in a crazy place in Las Vegas. The pastor was dressed as Elvis Presley.'

'I trust you will not want me to do the same.'

She whirled a gin and tonic into his hand and, leaning forward, gave him a hug. 'No, dear Nick, we want you to wear whatever you think suitable for the occasion.'

He raised his glass to her and at that moment Sir Rufus Beaudegrave came through the door. Nick stood up because he had been well brought up by his mother and was fanatical about good behaviour.

'My dear Sir Rufus, I hear that I am about to be called into service.'

'Are you?' He looked puzzled.

Ekaterina interrupted. 'I have told Nick our news. He has agreed to give us a blessing in the chapel.'

'Well, that's absolutely splendid. Thank you so much.' Rufus glanced at his watch and added, 'Sorry to be a bit late. The crowds were rather large today and I had something of a struggle to greet them all. But it's all good for business, I'm pleased to say.'

Nick metaphorically raised his hat to the effort that went in to keeping Fulke Castle in family hands. The unfortunate part about it was that Rufus's first marriage – to a titled airhead who had run off with the gamekeeper – had produced four daughters, none of whom could inherit the mighty place. There was a younger brother, of course. The typical ne'er-do-well who loved fast women – and the occasional fast boy, if rumour were correct – fast cars and fast living. He had been married three times and had a son by each wife. Fate was simply not fair, Nick considered. But now, with Rufus's remarriage there might yet be hope of an heir. The vicar sent up a rapid prayer that this pleasurable ending for everybody might be fulfilled.

Ekaterina rose from her chair. 'Where are the girls?'

Rufus smiled. 'I know that the youngest has gone out riding but the other three have all gone off to see friends.'

'Then I think I'll go and join the little one.'

'Do you ride well?' said Nick.

Ekaterina laughed joyfully. 'I'm not really any good. But Perdita is teaching me.'

'Then off you go,' said Rufus and gave her the tiniest smack on the bottom.

No need to ask how their relationship was progressing, thought Nick. One could tell at a glance that it was rock solid. Once again he spoke before assessing the words properly.

'I'm so glad you and Ekaterina are getting married, Sir Rufus. Let's hope it might produce an heir for you.'

The owner of the castle shot him a wry grin. ''Tis a consummation devoutly to be wished,' he quoted.

Having started, Nick could not leave the subject alone. 'And how about Ekaterina? Does she want children?'

'Does she!' answered Rufus laughing. 'I tell you, she is totally besotted with my daughters. In fact, she's a better mother to them than their actual one. And she would adore children of her own. They'll probably all turn out to be girls, but what the hell.'

Nick, sipping his second tonic and gin, thought what a truly nice man Sir Rufus was.

He changed the subject. 'I was wondering if you had any questions for me about the Grand Village Fair.'

'No, why don't you describe it to me.'

'Well the general idea is to make the whole theme medieval. We've hired a team of archers – I believe they're all amateurs but they're very good. They appear in films, that sort of thing. We've also hired a set of morris men—'

'The Casselbury Ring crowd?'

'No, they had another engagement. This lot are called Mr Grimm's Men.'

'Where do they come from?'

'Foxfield. Apparently they are a very ancient troop who disbanded after the Second World War only to reunite some ten years ago.'

'Not with the original members, I trust.'

'You trust correctly. This lot are quite young and vigorous. They even have a professor of history amongst their ranks.'

'I'm impressed.'

'Anyway, that aside, we're going to try and make the stalls

look authentic and all the stallholders will be dressed up, mostly in stuff from the WI pantomime, I'm afraid. But there it is. Anyway the beer tent is going to make some effort to look ancient and will be selling Ye Olde Ale and that sort of thing.'

'Sounds good fun to me. Now you'll want to know about the field I can lend you.'

'Please.'

'Well, it lies behind the Remembrance Hall and has the most exquisite view. It's lying fallow at the moment so I think a heavy duty mow or two should make it quite suitable for your purposes.'

'You think it will be big enough?'

'Oh, I should say it will be ample.'

'And how will people get in?'

'There's a rather rough path leading directly to it. I can get it cut back a bit if you like.'

Nick protested. 'No, I'll ask the chap who mows the graveyard to do it – and to mow the field too. You've done enough in giving us the space to hold the fair.'

'It should be quite a sight. Will visitors be encouraged to dress up?'

'It will be optional – you know the English.'

'Indeed I do. I went to a Lady Chatterley dance once and would you believe there was somebody all got up in a crinoline?'

'Yes,' Nick answered sadly. 'I would believe it. I have seen a great many strange sights in my time.'

'I'll bet you have.'

The door opened and in walked Iolanthe. Nick thought that in the relatively short space of time since he had last seen her, she had grown more like her father than ever. She had also grown up, looking at him through mascaraed eyelashes, her height quite considerable, obviously a Beaudegrave hallmark. Nick stared at her, a little nonplussed, never being quite sure how to treat teenage girls. However, she obviously was perfectly used to dealing with people who were shy.

'Hello, Reverend Lawrence,' she said, holding out a confident hand. 'How are you? I haven't seen you for ages.'

'I'm very well, thanks,' Nick answered, and shook it.

'Well, I'm going to dress up,' she answered, coming directly to the point and making no effort to conceal the fact that she had been listening outside the door. 'In fact, I'd like to help on a stall if that's possible.'

'Well, I can certainly ask if anybody wants any help. A lot of the volunteers are members of the WI. But the younger ones are quite go-ahead.'

'Don't you like the WI, Vicar?'

'I don't really approve of any organization that bans the other sex. Men's clubs, for example. But as individuals I think members of the Women's Institute are generally charming and hard-working and they are certainly doing their very best to help with the Medieval Fair.'

'It sounds terribly exciting. I wonder if I could help out the fortune teller.'

'I don't think we've booked one of those.'

'I'd love to do it if you can't find anyone.'

Sir Rufus spoke from his armchair. 'No, Iolanthe, you're far too young. I won't hear of it.'

'But Daddy, I'm fifteen. I'm not a child any more.'

Rufus lowered his newspaper. 'You will always be a child to me, even when I'm eighty and you are fifty. And it's no good wheedling because the answer will still be no.'

Iolanthe rolled her eyes and turned back to Nick. 'Then I'll set up a stall selling castle produce. We have tons of it in the shop. The gooseberry jam is particularly popular, by the way.'

And what she said happened to be true. The grand tour exited into the gift shop, which Rufus had established in a converted barn, selling everything from a booklet written by himself on the castle's history to wine and free-range eggs, with as many trinkets and souvenirs as he could pack in between. Its turnover played an important part in adding to the Fulke Castle finances.

'I think that is a very good idea,' said Nick. 'Would you agree to it, Sir Rufus?'

'My dear chap, I would agree to anything that would boost the funds and also help your fair along. Where did you say the profits were going?'

'To the steeple preservation fund. If we don't seriously rebuild it, it will come crashing down one day.'

'If you're having a raffle at any time you can add the

prize of a free balloon trip over the castle and surrounding countryside.'

'Thank you very much.'

They discussed the practicalities of Iolanthe managing a whole stall by herself and Rufus tactfully suggested that it might be so overrun with customers that Araminta should help as well. This she agreed to with a thoughtful nod, during which her marvellous mop of red hair flew round her head like an aureole. Nick was impressed and thought of suggesting to Ivy Bagshot that she step down from the role of principal boy in the WI annual pantomime and give Iolanthe a chance instead. Then he realized the folly of his ways and decided that discretion was all, if he wanted to stay on friendly terms with the parishioners of Lakehurst.

After refusing another drink, he was shown out by Sir Rufus's daughter and made his way round to the private car park. Glancing at his watch, he realized that he was late for his next appointment and drove rather faster than usual back towards the delightful but somewhat strange village of which he was the parish priest.

Returning to consciousness under a hedge was always an odd experience for Dickie Donkin because he was never quite certain which way up the world was. Under his back he could feel the earth, hard and uncompromising, while over his head there seemed to be a vast crown of thorns and leaves, all interwoven. What he always did in these circumstances was to blink his pale blue eyes – so pale that they looked like the sunlight glinting on a glacier – several times over. Then he would heave himself up on to one worn elbow and see if the world turned round again and then, when it didn't, clamber into an upright position and grasp the hedge with a hand on which was a mitten so old and tired that it looked like a tracing done by an angry child.

Dickie Donkin had been living rough for many years now and yet the view that greeted him when he finally stood on his worn and battered legs was always fresh. He would gasp at the neatness of the fields, at the beauty of the villages that lay in front of him, at the majestic splendour of the tall trees, at the wheeling and dipping of the birds in the sky above. Then his hand would go to the worn, old school satchel that he had stolen many years ago from a playground, fasten round the shape of a bottle he always carried within, and raise it to his lips. What was inside was anybody's guess – usually the contents of a can of cider transferred to the Scotch bottle to give him a feeling of importance, but sometimes a drop of gin that a publican would give him just to stay outside and sit solitary on a bench, supping, and sometimes it would be a lager or a pint. But whatever it was that he purloined or was given as a hand-out, the bottle was always full.

Dickie Donkin was known throughout the vast county of Sussex because he had walked its entire length and breadth in his time, starting when he was twenty and his mother had died. There had been something about the rent book – he didn't understand it – but apparently it could only be passed down three times. Whatever the facts of the case, he had found himself without a home and had quite literally been turned out on to the streets by his landlord. So he had taken to the highway and walked from that day to this.

A legend had grown up about him, about Daft Dickie Donkin, as he was known. A legend that it was lucky to get a sighting of him, that it brought good fortune to see him when one was out and about. Children would often run after him chanting, 'Smile at us, Dickie. Come on, look our way.' Sometimes he would oblige them, showing what was left of his rotting brown teeth in the parody of a grin. Other times, when he was moody or not interested, he would keep his pale eyes fixed on the ground and hurry away, conscious of their feet scampering in his wake. Yet he wasn't quite as daft as people thought. He knew a thing or two about folk, having observed them from a midnight tree or caught them in the long grasses. So he was also known as Dickie the Watcher and he preferred that name because it gave him a certain air of dignity.

This day, though, when he awoke and gradually got to his feet, he saw that a man sitting on a mower was cutting the long grass in the Nether Field, part of the grounds owned by some local toff. Dickie had walked forward, his gait long and rolling, and had stared silently. The man had waved an arm. He had heard the legend that the tramp was a lucky omen. But Dickie approached cautiously, wondering whether or not it was a trap.

'Hello, there,' the man on the mower called out. 'How you doing?'

Dickie remained silent. He rarely spoke, because he didn't care to. He had been born autistic. The only sound he liked was his singing and often at midnight, standing solitary in the woods, he would startle the night creatures by chanting to the moon in a rich, melodious baritone.

'Want a beer?' continued the other. 'I'll buy you one if you like.'

Dickie nodded.

'Do you know the Great House?'

Dickie nodded again.

'Well, start walking then. I'll catch you up.'

Dickie gave a deep nod to show he understood and proceeded across the fields, his gait now rolling and purposeful as he had just received an invitation and did not want to be late getting there. After a while the man on the mower passed him and gave a cheery wave, pointing in the general direction of Lakehurst. Daft Dickie raised his pale eyes but otherwise gave no clue that he had even noticed.

TWO

On Tuesday nights the Crossword Club met in the Great House for what should have been a convivial evening. The vicar, however, found it generally boring and stuffy, the men who belonged being elderly and over-hearty, prone to remarks like, '*The Times* were absolute stinkers this week. Or at least that was how they struck me.' Then there would be a general murmur of consensus with, perhaps, one dissenting voice.

On this particular night Nick's head was full of the Medieval Fair and he had been held up on the phone by the captain of Mr Grimm's Men, Chris O'Hare, arranging to arrive on the day at nine in the morning in order to get a look at Patsy Quinn, who was opening the fair at ten o'clock. She was the sort of girl that Nick considered ghastly but for all that had come fifth in the *Britain's Got Stars* contest a year or so previously. After this she had formed a band and sung loudly on a C tour of the British Isles. Her only claim to knowing Lakehurst was that her grandmother lived there and the organizing committee had rather desperately agreed that she should open the fair if she was free. Inevitably, she was.

Not feeling in the least like socializing, Nick nonetheless made his way to the Great House to find the various members of the club at odds with each other.

'I say the fellow ought to be moved on. He's occupying that bench at the bottom of the garden and is definitely sleeping there. God knows what his sanitary arrangements are. I think it gives the village the wrong sort of image.'

'Hear, hear!' said the local bank manager, who had a quite uncanny resemblance to Captain Mainwaring.

'What's all this?' said Nick, feeling irritable.

'Some old tramp has taken up residence on the seat at the bottom of the Great House garden. He just sits there staring at the view. I have spoken to Constable Littlejohn but he says the fellow's an old Sussex character and will move off of his own accord in a day or two.'

'Well then, what's the problem?'

'This is an historic Sussex village, Vicar, and a tramp sleeping on a bench is not the kind of thing that should be encouraged.'

'I suppose if Christ came and sat on the bench beside him you would accuse him of being an illegal immigrant.'

There was a rather fraught silence.

'Perhaps you could talk to the man, Vicar. He might listen to you.'

'I have no objection to that whatsoever,' said Nick, and marched out of the pub's side door and down the length of the beautiful garden.

It was just getting dark and Nick slowed his pace and looked at the exquisite view opposite, drawing in a breath of delight as he always did. The garden sloped gently downwards and ended in a lane with pretty cottages built on either side. Beyond these a hill descended, growing steeper as it approached a small brook, which bubbled, ice-cold and fresh, at the foot of the valley. But it was to the majestic sweep of the elevation opposite that Nick's eye was drawn. With the reflection of the sinking sun dappling it with shades of pink, it almost looked unreal, like the playground of the gods.

Daft Dickie, as predicted, sat on the bench, motionless, staring at the view as if he were taking in every detail, which perhaps he was. Nick silently slid in beside him, noticing the odour of the man, not altogether unpleasant, for he smelled of earth and hay and being outdoors.

'Evening,' said the vicar, but there was no reply, just a general quiet.

Nick stole a look at his companion and knew at once that there was something not quite right. He guessed at autism or some similar mental disorder.

'Would you like a drink?' he asked.

This time he was rewarded by a glance from a pair of eyes, ice blue in colour. The man nodded and turned his head in Nick's direction and the smell of old, sour alcohol hit him head on.

'Will you be staying here long?' the vicar asked politely.

For answer, Dickie got to his feet and began a low, rumbling song which the vicar vaguely recognized. His grandmother had sung it, accompanying herself on the piano, and it was entitled 'Come to the fair'.

To say that Nick was nonplussed would have been to under-state the case, yet there was something lovely and rural and jolly about the fact that an autistic man was on his feet, singing. For no reason that he could possibly state, Nick stood up and joined in, humming along when the words failed him. He felt rather than saw Daft Dickie Donkin's approval. Then, as suddenly as it had begun, it was over. Dickie turned and shuffled off in the direction of the pub's outdoor lavatory. At least the question about sanitary arrangements was answered. Nick, in a better frame of mind, went back into the Great House.

The Tuesday club were agog.

'Well, Vicar, did you see him off?'

'I didn't try to. He's a perfectly harmless, friendly soul. He uses the outdoor lavatory and does not leave litter lying about. But I don't think he likes company much and I expect he will move on tonight. There, does that satisfy you, gentlemen?'

There was a half-hearted shuffle of feet.

'I think it best that he was spoken to by somebody in an official capacity,' said the bank manager who looked like Captain Mainwaring.

'Hear, hear!' murmured one or two voices.

'Well, now I've done my Christian duty, I think I'll leave you to your crosswords. Forgive me, gentlemen, but I want to make the tramp the subject of my next sermon, so I'd better get on with it.'

As the door of the Great House closed behind him, he heard someone say, 'Odd fish, that one.'

'Doesn't quite fit in.'

Grinning broadly, Nick headed purposefully towards the warmth of the vicarage.

THREE

After a certain amount of deliberation the organizing committee of the forthcoming Medieval Fair had decided to make it a two-day event. At the urging of the Reverend Nick Lawrence it had been advertised widely, a considerable sum of money being laid out on bright, colourful posters which announced that it was going to be genuinely ancient with displays of archery and unrivalled morris dancing, together with stalls, pedlars and a fortune teller. These flyers had been distributed almost throughout the county with the help of determined folk driving great distances and pinning them to noticeboards. The die was cast. It was to be a two-day stint.

'Provided that we get sunny weather, of course. But with your help, Father Nick, that's a forgone conclusion,' said Mrs Ivy Bagshot, with a conspiratorial smile.

Nick had wondered how he was so supposed to perform the miracle but guessed that he was probably meant to have a direct line through to the Almighty.

'I'll do my best,' he replied in his customary manner, grinning cheerfully and looking reasonably confident. But within he questioned, as he did so often, whether God would bother with the minutiae of the Lakehurst fête or whether He was more concerned with problems more profound. Whatever the answer, he still sent a small, meek prayer for the weather to be fine as he walked into the Great House two days before the event.

Dr Kasper Rudniski, the latest addition to the stable of doctors who served the community, was still regarded as a new boy, despite having been in Lakehurst nearly four years. Nick had arrived in the village shortly after the doctor and the two of them had formed the sort of bond that strangers in a new environment frequently do. Now he was pleased to see the Polish man as he walked into the Great House.

'Hello, Kasper. Haven't seen you in a while.'

'No, we have a doctor off sick and I have been covering her duties.'

'Poor soul. Will you have time to come to our Medieval Fair?'

'I wouldn't miss it for the world. Are you having a maypole?'

'Yes. And hopefully pretty little children dancing round. Which reminds me, I've got the task of going to the school and getting a list of their names and who will be taking them to the field. I rather dread it, in a way.'

'Why? They're only kids.'

'I know, Kasper, I know. But they stare at me with unsmiling faces and I try to be jolly but they don't laugh at my jokes.'

'Well, I think that's sad. You're a vicar and you don't know how to handle children.'

Nick gave a sloping grin. 'I know. It's pathetic. But they scare me stiff.'

'You should go for hypnosis.'

'I think perhaps I will.'

'When is this terrible event to take place?'

'Tomorrow morning. Just after break time. They will file into their classroom to be greeted by me.'

'What a treat,' said Kasper, and smiled sweetly as he ordered a round.

Yet Nick felt genuinely nervous as he walked the short distance between the pub and the vicarage. Letting himself in, he told himself not to be idiotic as the smell of old wood and log fires greeted him, followed by the familiar feel of Radetsky, his cat, stropping round his ankles. After all, they were only children and he would give them a short talk on the origins of the maypole – omitting the fact that it was a phallic symbol and the dances round it were exuberant expressions of fertility. Very like the carol sung on the church roof on May Day, which Jack Boggis was still maintaining was an invention of the socialists.

Nick had just settled down to watch television when there was a knock at the vicarage door. Putting on a smile, he went to answer it. The leader of the group of morris dancers known as Mr Grimm's Men stood in the entrance.

'Good evening, Vicar. I was visiting a friend in West Street and thought I would call just to check a few facts with you.'

'Yes, of course. Come in, come in.'

'Nice old place you have here. I thought most vicarages were a bit modern and dreary.'

'Thank you very much. I was very lucky to get it, I can tell you. You've seen a few of them, then?'

'The group gets called upon for the odd village fête, so I have visited one or two, yes.'

'Well, Mr O'Hare, do sit down. Would you like a glass of wine? How can I help you?'

'Yes, please. And it's about what you want us to do at the fair.'

'Well, I was wondering if you could mingle with the crowd when you're not dancing.'

'That should be all right. As long as we can mingle in the beer tent.'

'Some of the time, certainly. But if you could chat up the visitors a bit? We're hoping that one or two will come in costume.'

'You'll be lucky.'

Perhaps because he was tired or perhaps there was something slightly odd about O'Hare but Nick was finding it difficult to make conversation. He was trying to think of something to say to the strange young man, with his peroxide hair and his pointy green eyes, when Chris spoke.

'Do you come from Sussex, Vicar?'

'No, I was actually born in Dorset. But my father's family lived in the west of the county.'

'We're all Sussex men – or should it be men of Sussex? – in the dance troop. That's how we got our name.'

'I don't quite follow.'

'Mr Grimm is old Sussex slang for the Devil.'

Nick stared, not quite sure how to answer, then said, 'Is it a joke?'

'Apparently not. Back in the 1500s when the group was originally formed, it had for its leader, one Thomas Hennfield, who was supposedly in league with Mr Grimm. The story goes that he fancied a girl called Alison Fairbrother but that she would have nothing to do with him. She was betrothed to someone else and was not interested. To cut a long story short, Thomas sold his soul to the Devil and Mr Grimm promptly removed his rival and Alison married Tom and had fourteen children. True or false, that's the story.'

'Rather a creepy tale.'

'Precisely.'

'And you've kept the name all these years?'

'When the group was reformed post-World War II, it was decided to keep the old title, despite its demonic connections. And it hasn't done us any harm. It usually causes a chuckle amongst the people who know what it means.'

'Well thank you for telling me, Mr O'Hare . . .'

'Chris, please.'

'Chris. It's a very interesting piece of folklore.'

'It is indeed. But there are some people who say that Mr Grimm is still practising his wicked ways in Sussex.'

'Do they indeed? Well, I'll just have to make it my mission to prove them wrong, won't I?'

Chris O'Hare made no answer but stared, eyes glinting, into his glass of wine.

Dickie Donkin loved walking in the woods at night. He liked listening to the sharp, cracking sounds made by the creatures as they moved from one place to another, foraging for food and hunting, or the great swishing of wings as the owls hovered over a poor wee mouse before gobbling it up. Every note that came from the forest sounded to his ears like a rustic rhapsody, a great harmonious burst of sound, and he was grateful to whatever it was that had turned him into a nightwalker so that he could enjoy alone this vast melodic symphony.

Standing by himself in a little clearing, thrilling to the great music he could hear, he put his head back and sang his appreciation:

All through the night there's a little brown bird singing
Singing in the hush of the darkness and the dew
Would that his song through the stillness could go winging—

He broke off abruptly as a different noise came like the sound of a saw through delicate fretwork. A car was driving down the lane nearby and drew to a stop a few feet away from where Daft Dickie was standing. The tramp faded into the shadows as there was the sound of the door opening and a man relieving himself.

Dickie felt annoyed that the beauty of the night-time anthem should have been shattered so rudely and wondered what he could do. He crouched down in one of the inkier patches of darkness and let out a low growl. He listened and heard the man hurrying to adjust his dress, noticing with satisfaction that the fellow's breathing had become shallow and nervous. Grinning, Dickie shuffled a foot closer and this time howled like a wolf. The cry rang out, deep and sinister. This time the man leapt into his car and drove off at speed.

Dickie laughed, a strangely sweet and melodious sound, and continued with his song, while the creatures of the forest stayed hushed to hear him.

FOUR

The next morning Nick rose bright and early and walked up the High Street then down East Street to where the Church of England primary school stood in all its Victorian glory, with one or two latecomers still hurrying inside. He had been asked to take morning prayers and was determined to try his best not to let his nervousness show. Striding manfully on to the platform in the wake of the headmaster, a weary man named Mabbit, Nick took the plunge and gazed out to where the children sat cross-legged on the floor. Fifty pairs of eyes stared at him glassily, all – or so it seemed to him – without expression. At least they aren't hostile, he thought, and gave them a smile. Nobody smiled back, with the exception of one little boy who looked as if he was part of another era with his long, floppy fair hair and large blue eyes. Nick was so grateful that he gave the child a broad grin, which was greeted with a faint laugh from someone or other. The vicar braced himself for the singing of hymns, during which his light baritone voice sounded loud, to say the least of it.

'Gladly, my cross-eyed bear,' he heard distinctly and glanced up to try and see the miscreant. A small girl with bobbing primrose plaits was looking so demurely at her hymn book that he decided it must be her.

Nick was called upon to lead the Lord's Prayer and could have sworn that he heard 'Harold be thy name' coming from the same source. He looked reprovingly but the child did not meet his gaze.

Afterwards he was ushered into a small classroom where a selection of the ten best dancers – as chosen by Miss Dunkley, who was in charge of Music and Movement – stood waiting tremulously. Nick was glad to see that the child with the floppy hair was present and was giving another tentative smile. He squatted down next to him.

'Hello, young man. What's your name?'

'Billy Needham.'

'I hope you're going to dance round the maypole at the fair.'

Miss Dunkley put in enthusiastically, 'Oh, Billy's a very good dancer – as are they all, Vicar. If you'd like to see them do their stuff, we've got a pseudo maypole in the playground. Would you?'

'Very much.'

They all trooped outdoors where a makeshift log had been placed in a Christmas tree holder. Someone on a ladder had pinned a series of colourful ribbons to the top and as a portable CD player suddenly burst into life, the children rushed forward, grabbed a ribbon and started to dance. They formed the most intricate patterns, the strands of colour crossing over then under each other. Nick was amazed and turned to Miss Dunkley eagerly.

'They really are awfully good. I presume you taught them all this?'

'Oh, yes. I'm a true history buff. I've read all about the maypole and the patterns you can weave with the ribbons. It's very interesting.'

'The dances were originally fertility rites, I believe.'

'Oh, yes,' said Miss Dunkley, brimming with gravity. 'They were indeed.'

Nick changed the subject, addressing the children. 'That was very good. Now will you be able to come for two days?'

They all nodded and there were little shouts of 'Yes'.

'And will your parents bring you?'

Miss Dunkley interrupted. 'I'll be bringing some of the children myself. And I shall stay as their chaperone, of course.'

'Oh, yes. Health and safety and all that.'

'And all that,' echoed Miss Dunkley in an undertone.

Billy piped up. 'Can I sit in the front, please?'

'Yes, darling. Provided you do up your belt.'

There was a very small buzz of 'Teacher's Pet'.

Miss Dunkley faced them. 'Will whoever said that step forward.'

A frenetic-looking child with challenging blue eyes and a mop of untidy dark curls stepped forward, then glared over her shoulder to see who else would have the nerve. At this a boy and the girl with the primrose plaits stepped forward.

Nick wondered if the teacher would dress them down here and now and was rather impressed when she did so, clearly not believing in the idea of delayed punishment.

'Chrissie, John and Belle, that was a very nasty thing to say. You know that Billy lives in the children's home in Mill Street because his parents are dead and I often give him a lift in my car. I happen to live in a flat nearby and it makes sense that I should pick him up on my way. He is not my pet – and neither are you three. In fact, I've a good mind to take you out of the maypole dancing team.' She turned to Nick. 'What do you think, Vicar?'

He was no longer ill-at-ease. 'I hate cruelty and unkindness and it was nasty to tease Billy. But I think on this occasion you should let the children continue to dance at the fair.'

'Very well. Say thank you to Father Nick, the three of you.'

The frenetic child would not meet his eyes, growled her thanks and went back to the rest of the class, the boy the same. But the little girl with the swinging plaits gave him a polite curtsey, a sweet smile and said, 'Thank you so much, Father Nicholas. You have been very kind to me,' before she rejoined her playmates.

Walking with the teacher as the children hurried back into their classroom, Nick asked about her.

'Oh, Belle? A pretty little thing, isn't she?'

'Very polite, I thought. Unusual these days.'

'She's brought up by her grandparents, you know. Her mother and father were killed in a terrible road crash. Miraculously she escaped. It's rather pathetic. She calls them Mummy and Daddy.'

'Poor little girl.'

'Oh, she has a very good life. They indulge her every whim.'

'Wait a minute. Is her grandfather Major Wyatt? Mid-fifties, rather a good-looking man?'

'Yes. Do you know them?'

'I called at their beautiful house once on a pastoral visit. He was in but his wife and the child were out. He told me that they didn't go to church but offered his help with any events we were running. In fact, he and his wife are manning a stall at the fair.'

'I shall see them there, then.'

'I do hope it's going to be fine,' said Nick, and Miss Dunkley patted his arm and said she was sure it would be.

* * *

Dickie Donkin was thinking. He was remembering his mother, who had looked like Mrs Noah except that her eyes had been like violets and not the dark, snapping ones of the wooden toy. He remembered a huge fist crashing into her face, rearranging her features, sending her flying to the floor crying out 'Stop! Stop!' He remembered crouching over her and receiving a barrage of blows to his head. He remembered punching as hard as he could into his stepfather's crutch, making him bend over and gasp for air. The last thing he remembered before waking up in hospital was a great boot kicking him violently in the head.

His mother had been taken in to a home after that last and most vicious attack and Daft Dickie, leaving hospital, had slipped through the net of authority and gone to live rough, earning a pound here and there by chopping wood or helping farmers with the animals or anything else he could turn his hand to. But one night, when he was about twenty, he had crept back through the darkness to his old home and spied his stepfather in a drunken stupor, sitting in the rocking chair by the fire, mouth gaping, snoring thunderously. It had given Dickie enormous pleasure to creep up behind him and slit his throat from ear to ear, then turn and run like the wind, dumping his bloodstained clothes on the way and taking up his position in the barn where he slept and, to be sure that Farmer Packham had to wake him up in the morning, dressed in his son's old clothes, sleeping very deeply.

The police had questioned him, of course, but the farmer had sworn that the young man had slept in his barn all night, that the new clothes he wore had been given to him by the farmer's son. They had been suspicious – very – but had not been able to make a case. As for the bloodstained clothes, they had sunk beneath the waters of one of Sussex's reservoirs, helped on their journey by a brick, and young Dickie Donkin had ambled out of the police station and on with his lovely, singing, journey through life with never a backward glance.

FIVE

It was the day before the Lakehurst Medieval Fair and Mr Grimm's Men were having a very jovial rehearsal. This was in the courtyard of The White Hart in Foxfield and was accompanied by beer drinking and a great deal of hearty laughter. To regard them from a distance one could admit to thinking them a scary-looking bunch. For not only did they wear the black tatter-coats but also their faces were blacked up, hidden, nothing but a pair of eyes gazing out on the locals who had come to cheer them on. Atop this fantastical garb they wore black top hats with a mass of long feathers sticking up beyond the crown. The older villagers, whose parents remembered them pre-war, had passed down a tradition that one should never look a member of the morris team full in the face for fear of bad luck, but to the local youth, with their Mohican haircuts and their louche girlfriends, that was all a load of bull.

The morris musicians – two drums, a fiddle and an accordion – changed rhythm and Mr Grimm's Men engaged in a fierce overhead battle, beating sticks one against the other in a menacing manner. An old-timer, who happened to smoke a pipe and thus was banished out of doors, dropped his gaze and stared into his beer tankard at this point.

'What's up?' asked Kyle, a pimply boy of about nineteen.

'Don't like it when they do this part,' the old man muttered, still looking down.

'Don't tell me you believe all that Satan rubbish, Stanley?'

'This be the calling up. And I never watches that.'

'You've had too many pints, that's your trouble.'

'You'll learn, young feller. Never watch Mr Grimm's Men when they do the summoning.'

Kyle laughed and turned back to his fellow louts but Stanley kept his head down until that particular dance was over.

The dancing session done, Chris O'Hare marched his men into the hostelry and claimed the round of free beer provided by the landlord. The morris dancers' blackened lips fastened themselves round the rim of their pints and all supped deeply. There were twelve of them, ranging in size and age from Little Willie, aged twenty-one, to Old Elvis, aged sixty-three. In between those two were a variety of men all drawn together by a love of exhibitionism and a general enthusiasm for dancing and showing off. There was a Will and a Harry, a Joe and a Larry, not to mention Dan, Fred, John, Tom, Len and Keith. Despite the rumours, only a few of them were interested in the Black Arts, led by the redoubtable Chris O'Hare, who had dabbled with a bit of serious witchcraft in his time.

Without his black make-up he looked a little devilish, being blond as vanilla with a pallid skin and enormous, slanting tiger's eyes. For some reason women found him irresistible and flung themselves at him, which some thought was due to a spell he had cast in his youth. He remained unmarried and an experienced, excellent lover, well-hung.

'How many times do we have to dance at this Lakehurst thing?' Harry asked him.

Chris turned his tawny gaze in the man's direction. 'I reckon about twice. Morning and afternoon. But the vicar wants us to mingle with the crowd and be jolly.'

'I wouldn't mind mingling with Patsy Quinn.'

'Don't worry, Will. Chris will beat you to it.'

'If I can be bothered,' the devilish Mr O'Hare answered, and gave them all a broad grin to show there was no offence.

Mr Grimm's Men were making jeering noises when the longbow team from The Closed Loop came in. There were just four of them, all amateurs, who spent their non-working hours taking part in the recreation of famous battles and giving demonstrations in the art of archery. They were all members of the far larger and far more famous group, but had nothing against taking part in a local charity show. They were greeted fondly, having met on various occasions.

'How do, Reg? How's it going then?'

'Very well, I think. We've got the safety arrows ready for the general public to have a go and we're doing two demonstrations by ourselves.'

'What time are you getting there?'

'Just after nine. We want to have a look at Patsy Quinn.'

'Who doesn't?' remarked Chris O'Hare, and the new arrivals were treated to a free round of drinks by the landlord, a jolly chap called Charlie.

The vicar had hoped for a quiet night in but the telephone rang constantly. Earlier in the day he had walked up to the field and been very gladdened to see the Women's Institute out in force, arranging stalls and putting up bunting that might be considered to have a medieval look. He had worked with them for a couple of hours and during that time could have sworn that he glimpsed Dickie in the trees that grew nearby. But when he looked again there had been nothing there. Other than that, there had been no incidents and when he gazed round the field at six thirty, with the WI packing up and asking him what he thought, he could not praise them enough. He had called in at the Great House on his journey back, hoping he might see Kasper.

Jack Boggis was in his usual chair, talking, for once, to a rather elegant, grey-haired woman who seemed to have a mind very much of her own.

'I don't know about you, Mrs Platt, but I'm not certain whether all this archery business is any good for youngsters. I mean, when I were a lad my father used to cuff me over the head and tell me to get on with it.'

'With what?' asked his companion in an extremely educated voice.

'Well, with life. We didn't have any medieval nonsense to fill our heads. We used to have to concentrate on the three Rs.'

Mrs Platt had looked down her nose, an achievement that the vicar frankly envied.

'But surely you studied history?'

'Yes, but . . .'

'There is no but about it. The children will be given the opportunity to study the living past when they are allowed to participate in the longbow demonstration.'

Jack had supped his ale, his face going a little grey as he wondered how to counter this unexpected attack. His companion meanwhile had taken an elegant sip from her glass of dry white wine. The vicar, much amused, silently watched them.

'So I take it you will not be going to the Medieval Fair, Mr Boggis?'

'Well,' Jack answered uncomfortably, 'I might look in on it for half an hour.'

'I should hope so indeed. I think it will be highly educational and interesting. Besides, it is in a very good cause.'

'What's that?'

'The church tower fund,' answered Nick, leaning towards Jack's table.

'My God, haven't you restored that by now? You've been raising money since the millennium.'

'Hardly. I started the appeal and I've only been here four years. We'll be glad to see you there, Mr Boggis. Anything to help support the tower.'

Jack clutched at his dignity, attempting to look benign and failing. 'As I said to Mrs Platt, I might look in for a short while.'

'We'll be delighted to see you,' answered the vicar cheerily, and turned back to his pint.

Kasper had not appeared and Nick had finished his drink and hurried home, Jack Boggis still arguing with Mrs Platt and being thwarted at every turn.

No sooner had he sat down to supper than the phone started to ring, mostly people asking last-minute questions about the fair. Finally at nine o'clock it went for the last time – and this was a call that the vicar was delighted to receive. It was from Olivia Beauchamp, down in Sussex for the weekend from her flat in Chiswick. At one stage Nick had had rather romantic leanings towards the violinist but these had been eroded over the months and now here he was, aged thirty, and still unmarried.

'Nick,' she said in her husky, sexy voice, 'how are you?'

'My dear girl, how lovely to hear from you. Have you been away?'

'Yes, I've been doing a few concerts in eastern Europe. But I'm back now for several months.'

'Good, you must let me take you out to lunch. It would be so nice to see you again.'

It was at exactly this point that Nick heard a man's subdued cough in the background. So the delicious Olivia was not alone.

He paused and heard her whisper, 'You did that on purpose,' followed by a definite rumble of a laugh.

'Am I interrupting anything?' Nick asked politely.

Olivia laughed, out loud this time. 'No, I've just got a friend round for a drink. I really rang up to ask about the fair. What would be the best time to arrive?'

'Well, it's being opened at ten o'clock by Patsy Quinn . . .'

'Complete with piercings?'

'And tattooed up to the eyeballs. But I mustn't be unkind. Her grandmother lives in Lakehurst and she will be a big attraction for the teenagers. After that short ceremony, I presume I shall accompany her round the fair and that will be that. So come whenever you like. There will be morris dancing and archery and a fortune teller throughout the day.'

'I'll probably come about twelve.'

This time Nick heard the sound of someone getting up from a chair and knew from the very way it was done that it was not Olivia. His curiosity was as high as a UFO.

'That would be lovely,' he said, longing to add 'Bring your friend' but not quite having the nerve.

'See you tomorrow then.'

'I look forward to it.'

He put the receiver down and went to the kitchen where he made himself a cup of blackberry tea, puzzling over who Olivia's friend had been. Probably a Slovakian pianist, he thought, and with this happy idea made his way upstairs to bed. Just before he slept, Nick opened the window and looked out at the moon. It was waxing and was almost full. He strained his ears because from the lane at the back of the garden he could hear somebody singing.

I passed by your window in the cool of the night,
The lilies were watching, so still and so white.

Nick recognized the voice instantly and called out, 'Goodnight, Dickie.'

There was no reply, just the sound of someone creeping quietly away.

SIX

It was the day of the Medieval Fair and Nick rose at seven, showered, then dressed very carefully. He put on what he thought of as his tropical suit, a light-blue cotton cloth, which for some reason looked very dashing with a pale shirt and a dog collar. He also, as the weather was extremely fine, put on a panama hat and felt very sophisticated as he drove his car to the car park by the Commemoration Hall. From there it was a route march, down the winding path, then a short walk to the field where Nick saw hordes of women setting up stalls with enormous enthusiasm. He did a quick tour of inspection then hurried back to the car park, just praying that Patsy Quinn was wearing sensible shoes and would not have to stagger down the path on seven-inch heels. On the way he passed Sir Rufus Beaudegrave, complete with Ekaterina and the two elder daughters, all dressed in medieval costume.

'You look terrific,' Nick said, raising his panama.

And Iolanthe in particular was utterly beautiful, her great mane of red hair – exactly the same colour as Rufus's – falling about her shoulders, a somewhat inadequate cap pulled on over the top, her figure neat and delicate beneath the folds of her costume. Araminta, though so dark and different, was equally striking, while the great ageless beauty of Ekaterina, dressed in a Russian costume representing a Tsarina of centuries ago, glowed with the happiness of her situation.

The vicar spoke in all sincerity. 'You are a very lucky man, Rufus.'

'I know,' the other answered from beneath the folds of a wooden stall table which he was manhandling down the path.

'Can I give you any help with that?'

'No, I'll manage,' Rufus gasped. 'You'd better get back to the car park. There's quite a crowd gathering to stare at Patsy Quinn.'

Nick hurried to the top of the path to see that there were already about fifty people forming an untidy crowd round the

place where the cars drew up. Of Miss Quinn herself there was
no sign.

Mr Grimm's Men were already assembled and Nick felt a
sensation like a shiver at his spine as he looked at them, standing
so still and silent, not jostling like the rest of the mob but just
waiting quietly in their tattered black coats and top hats, their
features disguised, their instruments mute. Momentarily the
thought that they might still be practising the ancient arts went
through his mind with horrid clarity.

Noisily, the four archers arrived, breaking his mood, and Nick
started to play his part, shaking hands and talking to children,
who were arriving with their parents, Miss Dunkley gallantly
driving a minibus loaded with them. He noticed that the dignified
Mrs Platt, she who had put Jack Boggis in his place, was standing
by herself, looking both calm and composed. He went up to her.

'How very nice to see you again. Thank you for coming.'

'My pleasure. Actually, I'm waiting for Patsy Quinn.'

'I didn't think you'd be interested in her kind of singing.'

'Oh, but I am. Very. You see she's my granddaughter.'

Nick looked astonished. 'Really? I had no idea.'

'I thought you'd be surprised. But we are all musical, you
know. I used to be a very good pianist. But here she comes.'

The vicar afterwards thought, to his intense shame, that he
had been expecting anything between a rock chick to a latter-day
punk to a heavily pierced and tattooed being who stared out at
him from eyes drooping with false lashes and kohl. Instead, a
lovely girl stepped out of the small blue car and gave a deep
bow to the crowd, who roared in one voice. Nick was frankly
astonished.

She was beautiful in quite a different way, with short hair cut
close to the shape of her head. A pair of amber eyes, dancing
with light and widely set, looked out at Nick from beneath a pair
of dark eyebrows; her nose was beautifully shaped, her lips full
without that horrid fashion of appearing puffy and swollen. She
wore make-up, skilfully applied. She was, in short, a gorgeous
charmer. But one feature she had, which was quite inexplicable,
was that she appeared to walk in a glow, for there was a golden-
ness about her that was quite breathtaking. Mrs Platt stepped
forward.

'Hello, darling. How lovely to see you.'

Nick should have spoken but felt breathless and foolish so just stood silently while Patsy turned to the crowd who were surging round.

'How nice to see you all.'

Her voice was clear as a flute, with no annoying Estuary accent.

She started to sign autographs and pose for photographs and in Nick's mind a thousand mobile phones were raised to snap her.

'I hope you're all coming to the fair,' she called and turning to the vicar gave him a long, luxurious wink. To say that he almost fainted would have been a great exaggeration but he did have a definite churning in his stomach.

'And now I've got to do my job and start the festivities,' she said.

Nick at last moved forward. 'If you would like to take my arm, Miss Quinn.'

'How delightfully old fashioned – and how delightful.'

Arm in arm they walked down the path with a photographer from the local press running backwards in front of them. Eventually he slipped over a mound and both the vicar and Patsy Quinn had to help him up and restore his camera to him. He was somewhat elderly and sweating rather heavily. Patsy posed for one photograph on the promise that he would leave them alone if she did. Thankfully, he agreed, and stood aside while she took the vicar's arm once more and made her way to the fair.

Glancing round swiftly, Nick saw that all was ready, stall keepers standing behind their counters, maypole beribboned and fine, the archers' targets lined up and pristine.

'Excuse me a moment,' said Miss Quinn. 'Granny, have you got that bag I brought?'

'Right here, darling.'

'Then forgive a brief absence, Vicar. I've got a costume I want to put on. Where would be convenient?'

'In the beer tent. I'll ask the staff to step out for a moment.'

The crowd meanwhile were swarming down the path, children running, adults scurrying, the archers strolling and all to the accompaniment of the rhythmic beating of a drum. Looking to the back of the crowd the vicar could see Mr Grimm's Men, dark and sombre, their pheasant-feather headdresses lit up by the morning sun, making their way towards the fair. He wondered which one was the tiger-eyed Chris O'Hare.

Patsy Quinn stepped out of the beer tent to a smattering of applause from the stallholders. She had changed into a delicate medieval costume and looked exactly like Queen Guinevere, with a golden headpiece set on her brow and a purple overdress covering an underslip in pale lilac. There was only one more beautiful woman present, Ekaterina, and even she was challenged.

'I say. Bravo,' cried Nick and clapped enthusiastically.

The descending crowd joined in and so it was in the midst of thunderous applause and Mrs Platt wiping a moistness from her eyes that Patsy Quinn declared the fête open and immediately started to progress round the stalls. It was at the Beaudegrave Castle Produce stall that she spent most of her time, talking to the two elder girls and having a chat with Ekaterina. Nick thought how nice it would be if life could be like this all the time, full of colour and fun with everybody relaxed and enjoying themselves. But then he considered all the suffering and the pain caused by one nation to another in the name of religion and suddenly felt cross with his inability to do anything about it, other than try to be a good parish priest, a very small person in a very big and dangerous world.

With a sudden surge of the accordion and a roll of drums, Mr Grimm's Men stepped forward, their black tattercoats whirling in the sunshine of that glorious day as they began to dance a set which involved meeting in the centre and crossing to the end. The hobby horse – a new member as far as Nick could tell – stood at the side, moving its head occasionally to match the dancers' movements. It had a vicious-looking jaw and a set of big teeth which could frighten anybody if it should decide to chase them. Which is precisely what it did once the dance was finished, heading for Araminta Beaudegrave, who had stepped out of her stall the better to see. It was trying to drag her under its swirling skirts, which she was resisting as best she could.

Nick hesitated, not sure whether to go to her rescue or not. He took a few steps forward and a voice breathed in his ear, 'You leave Old Oss be, Vicar. He's only doing what comes naturally.'

He turned round. One of the black-faced dancers was standing beside him but who it was he could not be certain. And then he saw the glinting eyes behind the dark make-up and knew.

'I'm sorry, Mr O'Hare, but I don't see what is natural about frightening a girl out of her wits.'

'It's part of the maying ritual, Father. He's trying to take her under his skirts. Get it?'

'Yes, I do. But it's not right without her consent.'

Chris O'Hare gave a deep, low chuckle. 'Who knows whether she has consented or not? She must be eighteen or thereabouts. A full grown woman.'

'Well, I've had enough.'

And Nick strode forward but not as fast as Sir Rufus, who suddenly shouted in a voice fit to rally the dead, 'Leave her, Old Oss. She's not interested.'

The hobby horse spun round and stared at the speaker, then it snapped its horrible teeth and ran to the other side of the field where it stood pawing the ground. Nick had to laugh despite all the tension. Whoever was working it certainly knew just how a horse would behave. Meanwhile Araminta was acting in a grown-up manner and strolled nonchalantly back to her stall. Nick saw Iolanthe whisper something in her sister's ear and Araminta nod her head and giggle.

'Can you tell me how long I am supposed to stay?' asked Patsy Quinn, who had just emerged from the fortune teller's tent with a certain smile on her face.

'Why? Do you have another engagement?'

Patsy shook her head.

'You see, I was hoping that you – and your grandmother, of course,' Nick said hastily, 'might come back to the vicarage for a drink. Or a cup of tea. Or whatever you'd like,' he added lamely.

Patsy regarded him with a long, all-encompassing stare. Then she slowly put her hand on his arm.

'Do you know, I would rather like that,' she said.

Hidden by the trees, Daft Dickie was dancing a one-man morris.

> *Ha, ha, ha, you and me,*
> *Little brown jug, don't I love thee!*

'Now we fight with sticks,' he said to his non-existent partner, and he snapped off an old dead branch and whirled it over his head.

He sang lustily, his voice ringing out:

> *When I go toiling on the farm*
> *I take the little jug under my arm;*
> *Place it under a shady tree,*
> *Little brown jug, 'tis you and me.*

At this he leapt into activity once more and danced furiously round the forest clearing.

'What was that sound?' asked Patsy, cupping her ear.

'I didn't hear anything,' answered Mrs Platt.

'I thought I heard somebody singing.'

'Oh, that'll probably be Daft Dickie, our local tramp. Don't worry about him. He wouldn't hurt a fly.'

Before Patsy could answer him, Mr Grimm's Men went into a loud overhead battle, beating sticks together with much hilarity.

They certainly could dance, thought Nick, watching them narrowly. Knees high, booted feet pointing, they were masters of the craft. They ended the number by throwing their sticks high with a shout of 'Catch', which they proceeded to do, not one man failing.

'They're very good,' said Patsy admiringly.

'Did you know that Mr Grimm is an old Sussex term for the Devil?'

Patsy smiled. 'How quaint.'

'I suppose so. I always thought it a bit sinister.'

'Well, you're a vicar.'

'I don't see that that makes any difference.'

'Oh, but it does,' answered Patsy with much sincerity.

It was time for the archery display and literally dozens of people charged forward hoping to participate, Patsy Quinn included. Thus the vicar was left with Mrs Platt and was trying to make conversation when he saw Olivia coming down the path, her lovely smile beaming and her arms outstretched.

'Nick,' she called. 'Oh, how wonderful to see you.'

The next second she had thrown herself at him, knocking his panama flying, and kissing him roundly on the cheek. Over her shoulder he saw the man she was with and nearly dropped her as a result. It was Inspector Dominic Tennant, smiling with just the hint of a wink. Nick rapidly changed his mind about the Croatian pianist!

Dominic drew level and shook hands.

'Well,' said Nick truthfully, 'I didn't expect to see you here. Are you investigating anything?'

Dominic gave his pixie grin. 'No, just doing a little socializing. The fact is, despite its gory past, I like Lakehurst. Am I too late for the archery?'

'No, they're just starting. It's at the far end.'

'Right. Forgive me, darling,' and he dropped a swift kiss on Olivia's cheek.

A curtain which had been slowly lifting in the vicar's mind shot up to its full height.

'Well, well,' he said, almost to himself. 'So he won, did he?'

'What do you mean?' asked Olivia, giving him a sideways glance.

'Oh, a few years ago there was quite a gang of us . . . But you won't want to know about that. May I introduce you to Mrs Platt?'

'Of course, you're the violinist. Do you know I have a recording of you playing the Tchaikovsky? It makes me cry.'

From the butts came a shout as somebody scored a bullseye.

'Well, I'm going to the tea tent. Will you join me, Miss Beauchamp?'

'Will it be very rude if I say no? I would like to have a look at the various stalls and things first.'

'Of course,' said Mrs Platt, and swept away graciously.

Nick said, 'May I show you around?'

'Of course. Though I demand privacy in the fortune teller's tent.'

'Ah, another one.'

'What do you mean by that?'

Nick laughed, and told her all about Patsy Quinn and how she had ruined all his preconceived ideas of how a pop star should look and behave.

Olivia just nodded and Nick saw that she wasn't really paying attention, her eyes fixed on the amateur archers where the inspector was just testing the tensity of the bow.

In the forest Daft Dickie had climbed up to the bottom branch of a big oak tree to get a better sighting of unfolding events. He had thoroughly enjoyed the morris men and had afterwards ascended the tree to get a bird's-eye view of the arrows which arced through the air in a vivid display that made him – though only momentarily – want to be one of the longbowmen. When the kids took over he laughed loudly at that, thinking them a raggedy bunch of snotty-nosed varmints. But then had come the turn of the adults and he had particularly admired one girl in particular. Squinting at her hard he had realized that she was Queen Guinevere of storybook fame and a strange feeling possessed him, a sensation that was absolutely foreign to his nature. Just for a moment he wondered if he was Prince Lancelot – or whatever his name was – and then he became too interested in the arrows to think about it any more.

Yet that night, when he had made himself a den beneath the hedge, he thought of her, of the golden glow about her, of the way she had looked when she turned her head to speak to the long-bowman who was showing her how to pull the string, of the lovely bones of her face. For no reason that he understood, Daft Dickie began to cry, tears trickling through the dirt on his sad, weather-beaten cheeks. Then he remembered that he had a tin of cider in his pocket so he straightened his back and sang a farewell to the forest:

> *'Tis you that makes me friends and foes,*
> *'Tis you that makes me wear old clothes,*
> *But seeing you're so near my nose,*
> *Tip her up and down she goes.*

Then he drank the contents and settled down to a night's sleep in the hedgerows.

SEVEN

As it was the night of the fair, the Great House was packed with visitors as well as the regulars. Jack Boggis was looking extremely pained as some sightseer had taken 'his' chair and he was forced to sit elsewhere. To add insult to injury a passing customer had accidentally tipped a beer mug in the direction of his newspaper, leaving the *Daily Telegraph*, in a sodden condition. The greatest affront of all was that absolutely nobody was taking any notice of him.

Father Nick had stayed until the fair closed, somewhat amused by and definitely enjoying the company of Patsy Quinn. He had received the mildest form of tingling pleasure whenever Miss Quinn was asked for her autograph, and had gone on to wonder how many of the viewing public watched *Britain's Got Stars*. A lot, it would seem.

Having discreetly got rid of Grandma, Patsy had insisted on going to the Great House where she had been mobbed by a horde of eighteen to twenty-five-year-olds clamouring for her signature. Nick had received many appraising glances as he was obviously escorting her. Kasper had bounded up enthusiastically.

'Good evening, Nick. I was at the fair but couldn't catch up with you. Who is the glamorous Queen Guinevere?'

'Patsy Quinn.'

'I'm sorry?'

'That's what I thought. She apparently was a runner-up on a television talent show. But she's actually delightful. I'll introduce you when she stops signing.'

'It must have been a popular show.'

'Indeed it must.'

The door opened and Major Hugh Wyatt squeezed his way in. He caught the vicar's eye.

'Evening, Father Nick. That was a damned good event you organized today. I thought it went awfully well.'

'Hello, Major. I saw you scoring bullseyes in the archery contest. Couldn't reach you for a chat, I'm afraid.'

'Did you see Belle dancing round the maypole?'

'She was the little blonde one with her hair flying out, wasn't she?'

'Absolutely. Melissa was so proud.'

'I'm sure. I thought all the children were very good. Miss Dunkley must be a dedicated teacher.'

'Oh, yes, I believe she is. Belle doesn't like her but then she doesn't like being told what to do. A very strong-minded young lady is my granddaughter.'

'Can I get you a drink, Major?'

'That's very kind. I'll have half a bitter, please.'

Kasper spoke. 'How is Belle these days?'

'Very well. She doesn't really get ill. She's a remarkable child.' He lowered his voice. 'Tell me, who is the beautiful young lady that the vicar has been squiring round all day?'

'Apparently it is a Miss Patsy Quinn. I think she won a contest on television, or at least she was runner-up.'

'I came fifth, actually,' said a voice behind them, and both men turned to see Miss Quinn in all her resplendent loveliness, standing behind them. She held out her hand to them both. 'My connection with Lakehurst is that my grandmother lives here and I don't think the organizing committee could find anyone better to open the fair.'

They both began apologizing and Kasper said in his best Polish way, 'They could not have found anyone more beautiful if they had scoured the country.'

Miss Quinn laughed. 'Oh, you silken-tongued flatterer.'

At that moment the major's mobile bleeped and he withdrew it from his pocket and stepped outside. Nick returned.

'Where's the major?'

'His mobile just bleeped.'

'Oh, I see.'

Kasper said, rather too casually, 'Have you seen anything of Olivia?'

Nick could not help it, he simply couldn't, but the love of a good gossip rose within him.

'I saw her at the fair today – and guess who she was with.'

Kasper looked blank. 'I have no idea.'

'The Inspector. Dominic Tennant.'

'Good God. So he won.'

'Looks like it, yes.'

Patsy interrupted. 'Are you talking about Olivia Beauchamp? I know she lives somewhere near here.'

'She has a weekend cottage up at Speckled Wood.'

'I think one could say that about someone who has truly arrived.'

Before anyone could utter a word about this fascinating point, the major came back in, looking slightly pale.

'I'm sorry, everyone, I'll have to go. Apparently the cat has had a bad accident and Melissa needs the car to take him to the vet's.'

'What's the matter, do you know?'

'He must have caught his tail in something and he's bleeding profusely and the tail is hanging on by a thread.'

'Oh, go now,' said Patsy, with sympathy.

'What a terrible thing to happen,' said Nick, and absently downed the major's bitter in practically one swallow.

As soon as the car turned into the drive Melissa was out of the house carrying a cat basket.

'Oh, Hugh, thank God you're back. Poor Samba. I think he's dying.'

'I'll take you to Malcolm's surgery now. Where's Belle?'

'Oh, I called in Mrs Betts. She's sitting with her.'

'Good.'

The wheels screeched as Hugh turned the car rapidly in the drive and they set off for Lakehurst village where the vet had a practice in the High Street. An hour later it was all over. The unconscious Samba – minus a tail, the wound stitched and the blood flow stemmed – was back in the basket and they were heading for Wisteria Lodge, Melissa weeping quietly with relief, the major grim-faced.

'How did it happen?'

'I haven't a clue. It looked as if it had been cut to me. He must have caught it on something outdoors. Thank God I found him or he would have bled to death.'

'Where *did* you find him?'

'Collapsed in the garden. Oh, darling, it was like a murder. He was covered in blood, poor thing.'

'How did Belle take it?'

'Oh, she wept and howled. She seemed terribly upset. What with her and the cat, I hardly knew which way to turn.'

Hugh removed a hand from the wheel and covered one of Melissa's. 'Don't worry any more, darling. I'm back now.'

She gave him a loving squeeze in return. 'It's not just poor Samba, there was something else as well.'

'What?'

'That damned old fortune teller at the fair.'

'Oh, don't tell me you went to her.'

'Yes, I did. While you were in the beer tent.'

'Well, what did she say?'

'She actually told me about the cat and said somebody was going to hurt it.'

'Good heavens! Did she say who?'

'No. But she said we must be very careful. That there was somebody evil who hung round us, who wished us no good.'

Hugh slowed the car and parked it at the roadside. 'You didn't actually believe all that rubbish?'

'I tried not to – but she was so accurate about the poor cat.'

'Did she say anything else?'

'No, but she kept warning me to be on the lookout. Oh, Hugh.'

And Melissa, such a cool blonde who rarely gave displays of emotion, burst into tears. Hugh sat in silence, looking at her. He loved the very bones of her, had shared such sorrow and anguish with this attractive, kind woman that he had to control his own emotions not to cry as well. He knew, of course he did, that these fortune teller people just said anything to please at these country fairs, but nonetheless it was – odd. Why should she mention the cat, of all things?

He turned to Melissa and said gently, 'I think we'd better be getting back. Poor old Samba will be coming round soon and I'm sure he'd rather be at home than in the back of the car.'

Melissa turned to him and said, 'I really do love you, Hugh. You're so sweet.'

'Thank you,' he said gravely, and turned the keys in the ignition.

Returning to the vicarage much later that evening, Nick Lawrence – minus Miss Patsy Quinn, who had decided to spend the night at her grandmother's – felt tired yet tremendously happy. The day had been a triumph in every way. From Mr Grimm's Men to the little children whizzing round the maypole, everyone had aimed to please. The archery contest had been a triumph – and a naughty smile appeared at Nick's mouth as he recalled Inspector Tennant shooting arrows for all he was worth. So the police officer had made a move in Olivia's direction which had obviously been successful. A few days ago Nick might had felt a tinge of envy but the revelation of Miss Quinn's charm had changed all that. He had arranged to see her in church tomorrow morning and was very content with that.

Radetsky came through the cat flap and Nick suddenly remembered Hugh's tale of an injured cat. He looked at his watch and saw that it was too late to ring and enquire but wrote a note to himself to do so in the morning. Above his head William, his resident ghost, strode across the landing and Nick smiled to himself. All was well. But the minute he had that thought a nasty picture crossed his mind. He saw a cat lying injured and bleeding, its great eyes open and staring at the sky, and for no reason at all he felt a definite shiver of apprehension.

EIGHT

As had happened to him a few times before, Daft Dickie Donkin woke in the moonlight to feel something sitting on his chest. Yet even before he opened his eyes he knew that this was heavier than the usual rat or squirrel, a bigger creature, more like a dog fox or a full-grown badger. With great cunning – or so it seemed to him – he punched whatever it was hard and raised his eyelids simultaneously. There was a squeal and Dickie looked briefly into the face of a demon before the creature ran into the depths of the woods, letting out a high pitched yelp as it went. Dickie slowly staggered to his feet, muzzy with sleep and too much cider. By now the yelps had grown faint and pursuit did not seem like a promising prospect. Instead Dickie decided to walk through the woods and get the smell of its earthy familiarity.

The site of the fair, the big field which all day had been buzzing with people, was empty now, riven with shadows and black patches into which one would have to stare to check that nothing had moved. Only the maypole stuck out of the darkness, its ribbons wound tightly round its stem except for one place in which they bulged outward, quite a large bulge, but a very still bulge with an arrow protruding from it. An arrow that once had flashed through the air but now had found its eternal resting place. Eternal indeed.

With every step, Daft Dickie began to feel more alert, the noises of the night ringing in his ears like the strains of a mighty orchestra tuning up. He began to sing:

> *One day there sang a little bird*
> *From out the heavens blue.*
> *No sweeter bird was ever heard*
> *For, Love, he sang of you.*

Dickie began to sing the chorus which was a medley of 'Ahs', ranging up over some high crystal notes. His voice was good, unskilled but powerful. As he walked and sang Dickie thought of his grandmother, who had sat at the piano and sung all these tunes to him as a child, songs that would be with him forever. He recalled vaguely that she had been a professional singer but he couldn't remember much about it. Just this vision of her in a long dress, turned to face him, a flower in her hair. Then he thought of his mother and all he could see was the mash that was left of her face, with his leering stepfather, his hands in bunches, stooping over her.

Dickie sang more loudly to drown his memories but as he approached the field in which the fair had been held he suddenly grew silent. Why, he could not have explained. It just seemed wrong to him for his booming voice to fill the emptiness of what a few hours earlier had been a scene of such vivacity and life. Now, the great field was empty. The butts stood silently, the arrows all gone, which was a shame because Dickie would have liked to have had a try. Pulling the string back, feeling its tightness as you strained against the curve of the bow, and then the great rush of air as the arrow left and aimed for its target. And then suddenly he saw one. In this black and white moonlit landscape it was quite clear. Sticking out of a lump on the maypole. Just wanting to be pulled.

Cautiously Dickie began to circumnavigate the pole, in the belief that if he approached in a circular manner he would keep evil at bay. Eventually, though, the circles he walked got smaller and smaller until he ended up stationary. Standing this close he could see that the lump was tied to the maypole by the fact that the ribbons had been danced round so tightly that whatever had been in the way had become enmeshed. Dickie stared at it curiously.

It wasn't flat on the ground. In fact, it was about a foot off, and about three feet in length. It had an odd shape, almost human, Dickie thought. After staring at it for a while he decided that it was a cocoon, that a gorgeous butterfly was inside but that someone had shot it and now it would never spread its lovely wings. He reflected on the sadness of this and eventually tugged at the arrow quite viciously, angry with the killer, whoever it was. It broke, the top half coming away with a strange little sound. Looking down at it Dickie saw that it was dark, coated with a sticky substance. He stared at it, standing motionless, because he knew perfectly well that the substance was blood.

How it had gouted from that thick neck when he had crept up behind and slit the fat throat crossways. What pleasure it had given him to see the man start forward in his death throes before he had collapsed back into his chair, motionless. Yet pleasure wasn't really the word. It was a feeling of justice being done, justice for all Dickie's mother's little moans of agony, for all the kicks aimed at Dickie's blunt shaven head, for all the screams of the cat as his stepfather had wrung the life from the poor, blameless creature. How marvellous it had been to run naked through his beloved forest, his blood-soaked clothes in a bundle under his arm, how wonderful to feel the icy water close over his head. He had emerged cleansed and cold, the evidence sunk to the bottom, only a short sprint to Farmer Packham's barn lying before him.

But this was wicked blood. Somebody cruel had killed the butterfly – or whatever it was that was wrapped up in that cocoon. Suddenly Daft Dickie Donkin was filled with dread. He threw the broken arrow to the ground and, turning, ran back into the forest, where he found himself weeping with fear and horror as he made himself a nest of leaves and climbed into it and hid himself away from all the vileness in the world.

NINE

Olivia Beauchamp's phone rang at 7.27 the following morning and eventually a reluctant hand stretched itself out from the depths of her duvet to switch off the alarm. After some fiddling about with the clock, her dark head emerged from the pillow and sleepily took in the fact that it was the phone that was making the noise. She picked it up.

'Hello.'

'Sorry to disturb you so early, ma'am, but I wondered if Inspector Tennant might be with you.'

'Would that be Sergeant Potter?'

'Yes, Miss Beauchamp, it is. Is he there?'

'Unless he moved out in the night, the answer is undoubtedly yes. Just a minute while I wake him up.'

At the other end of the line Mark Potter grinned broadly. Good on you, he thought. And wondered if his boss had spent a really cosy night with the beautiful Miss Beauchamp, who had done much to raise the profile of the violin – and other things, no doubt.

'Hello.' The inspector's voice was incisive, not in the least as if he had been spending many hours in the arms of the adorable Olivia.

'Are you all right to speak, sir?'

'What do you mean, am I all right? Of course I am. What's the matter?'

'999 have had a phone call redirected to Lewes, sir. It came through at just after seven. Something very odd has happened at Lakehurst. They want us both there.'

'What sort of odd?'

'Apparently they've been having some sort of Medieval Fair . . .'

'Yes, I know about that. I went yesterday.'

'Then you saw the maypole, no doubt? Well, the caller said that there was a body attached to it. Been put there overnight. Uniform are on their way but they want us in charge.'

'Right. Pick me up at Olivia's in thirty minutes. I'll make myself presentable, I promise.' And the boss gave a light-hearted chuckle, which Potter was most amused to hear.

Forty minutes later he was ready, having spent ten of those saying goodbye to the violinist, who was amazingly calm about the whole situation.

'Will I see you later?' she asked from the folds of her cosy dressing gown as he went out through the front door.

'Not even a murder will keep me away,' he answered, vividly reminded of his marriage and the contrived casualness of his ex-wife, delighted to see the back of him as she was on her way to meet her lover. He turned in the doorway.

'Do you like me?' he said, meaning it.

'Just a little,' she answered, and gave him a broad wink that sent his heart zinging.

The Crime Scene Manager had already arrived with his team and the top of the arrow which Daft Dickie had thrown on the ground was being examined by forensics. There were figures in white suits crawling everywhere but so far the lump on the maypole remained untouched. Dominic stared at it with a critical eye.

'That looks like a small child to me.'

'I hope to God you're wrong.'

'It could be a dog I suppose,' said Potter lamely.

'That stood obediently on a stool while the dancers went whirling round it?'

'But why should a child do that?'

'I take your point, absolutely. Come on, Dave. Let's have a look at it.'

The Crime Scene Manager called to two members of the forensic team who cautiously began to cut the ribbons binding the sad little lump, meanwhile ensuring that they were hidden from any outside gaze – not that this would have been possible with every member of the public ushered off the field.

Despite his flippant tone, Tennant's heart was in his mouth as the body of a small boy was revealed, shot through the heart, a broken arrow still sticking out of that crushed little corpse.

'What in the name of heaven could have induced a child like that to stand on a stool and await his execution?'

'A dare, sir?' asked Potter.

'Pretty ghoulish one.'

'That's what modern kids are like. They see death so many times on TV and computer games and God alone knows what, that I don't think any of them take it seriously any more.'

But there was something so infinitely appalling about the child's pathetically small body, impaled to the maypole by the broken shaft of the arrow and awaiting the doctor's examination, that Tennant found himself averting his eyes. He didn't like child slayings – who did? – finding the fact of innocence so cruelly and rapaciously savaged, hard to bear. He was a rotten policeman, he thought, as he gulped away unshed tears. Potter, sensing something about his boss said, 'Poor little soul, eh?'

'As you say,' answered Tennant, giving a brief nod of his head.

Even the doctor seemed moved, the smile of greeting wiped from her face as she took in the horrible circumstances of death.

'My God,' she said quietly.

There was a momentary silence while the doctor bent to her bag. Tennant pretended to cough and surreptitiously wiped his eyes, and Potter thrust his hands in his pockets and stared round the field. Eventually the doctor looked up and Tennant saw that she had put on her highly professional face, which made her rather resemble a wasp in full flight. She approached the body and began by feeling it.

'There's no great sign of rigor mortis because he's so small, though I can detect some. I'd say he's been dead about nine hours, possibly an hour or two more.'

Tennant worked backwards. 'So this ghastly ritual was enacted at about midnight?'

'You think it was that? A ritual?'

'Yes. No. I don't know, Mark.'

'More likely to be someone playing at William Tell and the joke going horribly wrong.'

'That is certainly a possibility, but where's the apple? Look, don't let's jump to conclusions at the moment. But several things have struck me.'

'Such as?'

'The child was shot several feet above the ground. So he must have stood on something. Further, the killer must have gone down on one knee to do the shooting. We must interview that archery team as soon as possible.'

'There's something else, sir.'

'What?'

'There was more than one person involved in the killing. Whoever murdered this child must have wanted the ribbons wound back over the body when it was done.'

'Which would necessitate at least one person other than the killer.'

Potter shuddered. 'This has got to be one of the nastiest crimes I've ever seen.'

'Anything involving children is always pretty rough. But I agree, this one has some particularly unpleasant aspects.' Tennant turned to the doctor. 'Anything else, Jane?'

'The poor child died instantly as the arrow struck him through the heart.'

'I wonder who he is . . . was. There's probably some distraught mother phoning Lewes while we speak.'

At that very moment Tennant's mobile began to ring. He put it to his ear and walked slightly away. Potter could tell by the very slope of his boss's shoulders that the news was not good.

'There's a child called Billy missing from the Lakehurst Children's Home.'

'Age?' asked Potter.

'Five,' said Tennant shortly. 'Come on, Mark. Let's get over there.'

Dr Jane May looked up from her medical case. 'I'll do the post-mortem as soon as I can.'

Tennant nodded and asked the photographer for a print of the dead boy's face. Then, armed with a picture for identification, he and Potter left the field and headed for their car.

TEN

Dickie Donkin had finally fallen asleep in a ditch beneath a hedge full of bursting wild flowers, their combined scents blocking out the smell of blood. For that was what he had sniffed in the air when he had pulled the arrow out of the lump affixed to the village maypole. Or rather, the broken stump of an arrow. But whether there had actually been that sharp, heavy aroma or whether it had been a memory in Dickie's confused brain nobody would ever know. To him, though, it had been real enough and he had looked up at the pink moon above his head and felt the wetness on his cheeks before bolting into the forest determined to walk through the night and get away. Yet reality had been far from the dream. The fact was that the whole experience had unnerved him to the limit of his physical capability. Daft Dickie had sat down under the hedge and wept with a combination of physical exhaustion and a chill feeling of terror which had touched him like a finger from the grave.

Next morning's awakening had been more muzzy that usual. He had searched in his tattered pockets for something to drink, something to drive the chill out of him, but there had been nothing and Dickie was left with no alternative but to walk to the nearest public house and beg for a bit of cheese and a cup of tea from a kindly landlord. His route took him past the field and Dickie – who had determinedly kept his gaze in the opposite direction – stopped short as out of the corner of his eye, he glimpsed something blue. The place was swarming with coppers and ghostly, masked figures clad in white. Daft Dickie stopped short and stared.

An ambulance had drawn up at the far end and some men were carrying a small, black plastic bag on a stretcher towards it. Dickie knew, with a great leap of his battered brain, that there was a body in the bag and that the body was somebody small and defenceless. He wondered then whether he ought to go and tell someone in charge that he had been there last night. That it had been himself who had tried to take the arrow out of what he had thought was a chrysalis, only for it to break in his hand. But Daft Dickie Donkin had spent too many years on the run after his frightening brush with the police following the death of the creature that his mother had married. They had scared him then and they scared him now. Dickie was shuffling from foot to foot in indecision when he heard a noise behind him and, wheeling round, found himself staring straight into the face of the thing he dreaded most of all, a policeman.

Mrs Starkey had stepped straight from the pages of a novel by Charles Dickens. Hair scraped back into a steel grey bun, eyes with rimless spectacles, which magnified them into watery blue bulbs, an obviously false set of white teeth that looked as if they had belonged to someone from the Scandinavian countries. No one, thought Dominic Tennant, might be found more unsuited to looking after a bunch of needy kids, yet appearances could be deceptive. When the formidable dame opened her mouth she spoke with a soft, mellifluous Scots accent and gave as kindly a smile as her teeth would allow.

'How can I help you, gentlemen?'

Tennant spoke. 'Good morning, madam. I'm sorry to disturb you. I believe you are the superintendent of this orphanage.'

She nodded. 'Yes, if you care to put it like that. You see, we look after all the unwanted children that anyone wishes to put into our care. We have a real mix here. Autistic, spina bifida, totally deranged, all living alongside children who just aren't required in their parents' life. But I take it you are here on official business?'

Potter held out the photograph taken at the crime scene. 'I'm Detective Sergeant Potter, ma'am. And this is Inspector Tennant. Tell me, do you know this boy?'

She stared at it and lost colour. 'Why, that's Billy,' she said.

'Does he live here?'

'Yes. But his bed wasn't slept in last night. Has anything happened to him?' She looked at the photograph again. 'My God, he looks ghastly. Oh my God. Is the poor child dead?'

Tennant was at his best. 'Go inside and sit down, Mrs Starkey. I'll get you a cup of tea and send a WPC to sit with you. Now who is your deputy here?'

'My husband. Not that he's much use. It's Ned really.'

'I hear my name being taken in vain,' said a bright Australian voice and Ned, who turned out to be six feet four inches tall and built like a Roman gladiator, appeared in the entrance hall.

He took over instantly and ushered a weeping Mrs Starkey into the kitchen, organized the making of tea, sent a message to the sleeping Mr Starkey and returned to where the two policemen awaited him in what was known as the parlour.

'Well, gents, this is a turn up and all. Now what do you want to know about our Billy? Poor little bugger.'

'You are aware that the wretched child has been murdered?'

'No, I didn't know that. Well, for Christ's sake! Who'd want to do a thing like that?'

'That's what we're trying to find out,' Potter answered. 'Now, sir, could you tell me something about this home and about Billy in particular.'

'Yeah, sure. Well, it's fee-paying as you will have probably guessed. Mrs S. makes a lot of dough through it. Mind you, she fair works her arse off for it. Some of the kids are quite crazed, let me tell you. Screaming and shouting and punching. Shit, it gives me the creeps.'

'And what is your role here exactly?' asked Tennant.

'Me? Well I'm just backpacking round the world and ran out of money. Saw an advertisement for this place and took the job for six months.'

'So you've no previous training?'

Ned shot him a look from under a pair of impressively dark eyebrows. 'No, I haven't, as it turns out. But I've got a way with the kids and that's undeniable. You ask the Starkeys.'

Potter spoke up. 'We're not questioning that at all, Mr . . .?'

'Just call me Ned.'

'Not Kelly, by any chance?' quipped Tennant.

Ned peered at him, saw that the inspector was smiling and grinned himself. 'Now he was a naughty boy. But he's regarded as something of a Robin Hood in Oz. All I can recall of him is an ancient film with Mick Jagger wearing a bucket on his head. It was a sight that haunts me.'

'I'm not surprised. But, that apart, we are here to ask some questions about Billy. You know who we're talking about?'

'Yes, poor little bastard. Billy Needham. He was just dumped here, you know. Which shows the contrast in different people. His parents were killed in a car accident and his uncle, a total wanker in my opinion, just dumped him on us, paid the fee and motored off. He sends a cheque every term and never shows up. Now Billy's school friend, young Belle, had just the same bad luck but her grandparents have given her a wonderful home and spoil the kid rotten. Life's a bitch.'

'Yes,' said Tennant reflectively. 'It certainly can be. Now, Ned, did you spend last night here or was it your time off?'

'No, I was here. I was on duty till eleven, which means I sat at the night desk at the bottom of the stairs. Then Rob Berry came to do the late shift and I went out for a walk.'

There was an unspoken quickening of interest.

'Where did you go exactly?' asked Potter, who had been writing in his notebook throughout the conversation and now gave Ned a glance which was meant to be nonchalant but instead was steely, making the Australian think that the young man still had a lot to learn from his boss.

'Just out to get a breath of air and have a fag.'

'In which direction did you walk?'

'To the left. Towards the fields.'

'Did you see anybody?'

'Yes, I did as a matter of fact.'

'Who was that?'

'First, a girl I didn't recognize, except that she was in fancy dress.'

Tennant sat forward. 'What sort of girl? Can you describe her? It would be helpful.'

'To be honest with you, I barely did more than glance at her. But I thought it well odd that she should be out walking on her own dressed like that.'

'Like what?' said Potter.

'Sort of elfin style. A long, flowing dress made of some light colour. Like a kind of hippie.'

'Was she tall or short, fat or thin, fair or dark?'

Ned looked at them reproachfully. 'Look, fellas, I only walked past the girl. I didn't stop and talk to her. I just got an impression as she went by. I'm sorry if I'm being difficult but that is truly all there was to it.'

Tennant leaned forward. 'Don't worry, Ned. If you do remember anything further please ring me on this number.' He passed a card. 'Now, was there anybody else?'

'Yeah, Chris O'Hare. All got up like a dish of fish in his morris man's outfit. Gave me quite a start actually because he was standing stock-still. I thought for a minute that it was a scarecrow until he spoke to me.'

'What did he say?'

'Nothing much. Asked if I had been to the fair and what I thought of it. I said no, I was planning to go today.'

'Are you sure it was O'Hare? I mean they all look very alike, especially with that black make-up on.'

'Yes, it was him all right. I recognized his voice.'

'Well, thank you very much, Ned. I take it that you saw no one else?'

'No, that was enough for one night. After that I turned round, came home and went straight to bed.'

Outside, in the car, Tennant said, 'I wonder who the woman was.'

'Got anyone in mind?'

'No. Nearly all the women at the fair – including Olivia – made an effort and dressed up. There were tons of females in flowing frocks around.'

Potter looked puzzled. 'Well, we'll have to wait on that one.'

'At the moment I'm more interested in Mr O'Hare.'

'Sounds a bit of a weirdo to me.'

'They all are. All of his troop. The scariest bunch of morris men I ever set my eyes on.'

Dickie Donkin had had a bad fright because the young policeman had stopped him and asked him what he was doing. He had made no answer but had just stood with his body in a poor little imitation of being at attention.

'It's all right, mate. I'm not going to hurt you. What were you doing hanging round here? This is a police cordoned-off area, you know.'

Dickie had hung his head but made no answer. The constable had peered at him closely.

'All right. I'll let you off this time but you'd better scarper. Vamoose. Go and find some other woods to hang about in.'

Dickie's arm had come up in a semblance of a salute then he had turned and sped off in the direction of Foxfield.

The constable had smiled to himself. He had a cousin who was born autistic and the signs were all too familiar to him. Having watched Dickie's retreating form, he had continued his steady tour of the woods.

'Poor catkin,' said Belle, her tears flowing freely down her pale cheeks. 'Poor little catkin.'

Melissa was busying herself around the Aga, making an apple pie which Hugh was very partial to. She had placed Samba's basket close by so that he could feel the warmth and Belle was getting in the way every time she opened the door.

'Darling, do you have to sit quite so close?' she remonstrated.

'Oh, Mummy!' The face turned towards Melissa was one of tragic reproof. 'I'm only trying to comfort my poor cat. How *could* someone do a terrible thing like that to her?'

'Darling, he might have been run over by a car. We don't know that it was a person.'

'But the vet said—'

'The vet said it looked more like a cut but he couldn't say what the actual cause was.'

'Can I see the stump?'

'No, you can not. The vet has amputated the tail and bound the remainder up. You are not to touch it, do you hear me?'

For answer Belle rose to her feet and stalked out of the kitchen, tears pouring freely. Melissa gave a loud sigh. If that had been one of her own two boys she would have shouted at them to go into the garden and do something useful, but Belle was different. She was a girl, she had an adorable face, and above all she was sensitive. Melissa fought down an impulse to run after her grand-child and comfort her. But one had to show authority sometimes, she told herself. Instead she continued to busy herself in the kitchen, tripping over the small stool which was not in its usual place. She picked it up and as she did so there was a strong aroma of bleach. She supposed that Hugh must have spilled something on it and set about cleaning it up. Then she thought of poor Samba and suspected that he had perhaps bled on it.

When Hugh had returned from Afghanistan, sickened by the killing and mutilation of his gallant and youthful soldiers, he had got a part-time job doing other people's gardens. The number of widowed ladies and elegant divorcees who employed him spoke for itself. But Melissa never doubted for one minute that Hugh loved her and her alone. Meanwhile he cheerfully pulled up weeds and pruned roses and was out of the house for several hours a day. Melissa thought that their way of life was to be highly recommended and with a smile on her lips arranged some flowers in a vase, then picked up a magazine. The telephone ringing broke her cheerful mood. It was a man's voice, light and well-spoken.

'Hello, could I speak to Major Wyatt, please.'

'I'm afraid he's out at the moment. Who is this?'

'My name is Tennant. I'm from the Sussex Police.'

Melissa's knees buckled. The memory of how she had been informed of the ghastly crash, of which Isabelle had been the sole survivor, dropped over her like a black hood. She felt her way to a chair and crumpled into it. The man spoke again.

'Are you all right?'

'Yes,' she gasped.

'You're clearly not. Just hang on a second or two and I'll come to see you. My car is very close to your house.'

'What's it about?' Melissa's voice sounded like somebody else's. 'Has there been an accident?'

'No, not at all.' Tennant was being ultra urbane. 'It's just about a school friend of your granddaughter's. That's all.' He rang off before she could ask another question.

Despite the early hour Melissa went to the sideboard and poured herself a weak gin and tonic.

By the time she had consumed it and was contemplating a refill, Tennant was knocking on the front door. She contemplated him instead. A good-looking man of about forty, with twinkly green eyes and rather long curly hair. He was holding his iden-tification badge, at which she stared blankly.

'May I come in, Mrs Wyatt?'

'Of course.'

'I'm sorry if my phone call upset you. It's not bad news as far as you are concerned. It's about Billy Needham, a school friend of your granddaughter. I'm sorry to say that the poor child was murdered last night.'

'Oh, how horrible,' said Melissa, going white as a cloud. 'Where did this happen?'

'At the fairground, after everyone had gone home.'

The door swung open at this point and Isabelle stood in the entrance. 'Oh, Mummy,' she said pathetically, and bolted into Melissa's arms, burying her face in her grandmother's shoulder, her small body heaving.

Tennant, who was not terribly good with children, wished that Potter was with him, and cleared his throat uncomfortably. He had the horrid feeling that he was watching a play and rather wished that he hadn't called.

Over Belle's head Melissa gave him a meaningful look, adult to adult as it were, and Tennant rose from his chair.

'Perhaps I had better come back at a more convenient time.'

'No, no. Please stay. I'm sure Belle will be calmer soon.'

The child, weeping profusely, muttered something in her grandmother's ear and Melissa hurriedly took her out of the room, presumably into the downstairs loo, from which direction came juvenile retching sounds. Tennant scribbled a note on the back of his card. 'Will return at a better time. Do ring me,' and made a hasty exit through the front door and into the safety of his car.

ELEVEN

Having caught up with Potter, who had been allotted the unenviable task of informing Miss Dunkley, Billy's teacher, of his death, Tennant and his sergeant made their way to The White Hart at Foxfield, partly because they were in need of a drink and partly because they had been advised that Chris O'Hare made a regular evening visit.

'Miss Dunkley was in an awful state,' stated Mark, drinking a St Clements without any relish at all.

'Why in particular?'

'She adored the boy, used to take him to the cinema and on outings. She was like an adoptive mother to him.'

'No chance of the relationship turning sour? Of the child doing something which might have driven her to murder?'

'Highly unlikely. She was genuinely distraught, as far as I could see.'

'As was young Isabelle. The wretched child was throwing up.'

'Not over you?'

'Perish the thought. Her grandmother removed her just in time.'

Potter grinned. 'I wonder how you would have felt if it had been your child.'

For the very first time, Tennant had a mental picture of himself as a family man surrounded by two or three small people for whom he was responsible because Olivia was away on tour. He quite liked the idea.

'I suppose I would have coped.'

Potter actually laughed. 'I can't see it somehow, Boss.'

Tennant let it pass but the seed of an idea had been planted. At that moment the pub door opened and a man came in with such strange but striking looks that both policemen turned their heads to stare at him. His hair was so blond that it was almost white.

'Looks like Boris Johnson,' said Potter under his breath.

Tennant guffawed loudly and the man looked directly at him with a pair of glittering eyes that were set in his face on a slant, giving him a slightly faun-like appearance. If Dominic Tennant had been anyone other than the character he was, he would have worried about the man being quite capable of coming up and punching him. He stood up.

'Chris O'Hare?' he asked.

'You're looking at him,' the other man replied with a sneer in his voice, and turned to the bar, saying loudly, 'A pint of Guinness, please.'

'That your usual tipple?' Tennant asked pleasantly, joining O'Hare at the bar.

The other raised a laconic eyebrow. 'Yes. Any objections?'

'You don't have an Irish accent.'

O'Hare looked down his nose. 'My great times three grandmother was burnt at the stake in Ireland for witchcraft. Her son fled to Sussex before they accused him as well.'

'I thought witches were hanged.'

'Not by a mob baying for blood. They'd build a fire and chuck you on it soon as look at you.'

'It all sounds very bloodthirsty.'

'It was, you can believe me. But why are you so interested? Are you a cop?'

Tennant produced his I.D. 'Yes. Why didn't you leave the fair after it ended yesterday?'

'I did if you must know. I went to the Great House and tried to chat up Patsy Quinn but I couldn't get a word in. The vicar and his cronies surrounded her all the evening. I've never seen a randy clergyman before. It was quite interesting, I can tell you.'

'So what did you do when your attentions were ignored?'

'I found someone else to talk to.'

'And might I have her name, please.'

'You could if I knew it. She called herself Skye but that was obviously a lie. She wasn't a Skye sort of person.'

Potter, who had left his chair and joined them at the bar, said, 'What do you mean?'

'Her voice was too cut-glass. She came from somewhere posh.'

'And did you spend the night with this top-drawer maiden?'

'I tried it on but no chance.'

'So that was what you were doing standing still while a nymph in a flowing dress walked away from you?'

Chris O'Hare looked startled. 'You're very well informed.'

'We're detectives,' said Potter with a smug smile.

'And I possess my ancestor's ancient powers, you know. Don't push me too far or I'll lay a curse on you,' O'Hare answered.

'Did you lay a curse on Billy Needham last night? Is that what killed him?' Tennant asked, looking serious.

'I heard the child was dead later this morning. But I can assure you, Inspector, that my coven does not threaten children.'

'How did you hear?'

'I run a garage outside Lakehurst. I open on Sunday mornings to sell petrol. The first person in was Mrs Ivy Bagshot. She was buzzing with the news.'

'Of course. She was one of the stallholders. About six of them saw the maypole and sent for the police.'

'It's a village, Inspector. The grapevine throbs constantly. Without it they would die of boredom.'

'Well, thank you, Mr O'Hare. We are setting up an incident room in the local school. I wonder if you would mind coming in tomorrow and making a statement.'

'No, I'll do that. I have nothing to hide.'

And with that the devilish man with the impossible hair turned to the bar.

The Vicar of Lakehurst had had an almost impossible day. Waking, flushed with the success of the fair and with the thought of Patsy Quinn accompanying her grandmother to church, he had whistled round the house and had picked up the phone with a cheery, 'Good morning. Lakehurst Vicarage.' The voice at the other end had been like plunging into a pail of icy water.

'Oh, Vicar, Vicar. The fair has been cancelled in the most horrible circumstances.'

'What? Why, Mrs Bagshot?'

'Oh Father Nick, it's too horrible . . .' And there was the sound of muffled sobs and a great deal of nose-blowing from the other end before the receiver went down.

Nick thought for a minute before dialling the number of somebody sensible, his old Polish friend, Dr Rudniski. As it was Sunday Nick guessed that he would be off duty but on call, so phoned even though the hour was depressingly early.

Kasper said his name in a wide-awake voice.

'My dear chap,' said Nick, thoroughly apologetic. 'Have you heard the news?'

'About the murder? Yes, indeed I have. Jane – the doctor – has just come off shift and came round for a quick coffee and a catch-up.'

'Well, who's been murdered?'

'A small boy. The police haven't identified him yet but rumour has it that it's Billy Needham. You might have seen him when you went to the school?'

'Yes, I have seen him. I know who you mean. Sorry, Kasper, I must go.'

Nick hung up abruptly as a vision of the sad face of Billy Needham danced before him. He remembered the lost look in the child's eyes, his lock of fair hair that fell over his brow, the fact that he was the butt of the children's cruel jokes.

'Poor little soul,' said the vicar, and found himself on his knees praying that the child who had so very little in life might have been better received on the other side of living – wherever that might be. How long he stayed like that he was not sure but a glance at his wristwatch told him that it was time for early service and he rushed across the road and into the vestry.

In the inexplicable way that villages have – Nick was still trying to work out quite how it was done – there was a tangible air of suppressed gloom. There were few people present at this initial service, held at 8.30, but even though it was too early in the day for any real evidence, the villagers already knew that the police were up at the field and that something terrible had happened there. In fact, one of the women in the congregation, Mrs Lynch, had been a stallholder and was also a member of the WI. It was really not that difficult to make the connection.

Nick decided to include some prayers for the occasion.

'Oh Lord, we beg that the soul of the recently departed be received into the company of the saints – and that somewhere there might be a little game for him to play.'

He didn't know why he'd said it, it had slipped out of his mouth because he was thinking it so hard, and he most certainly hadn't wished to poke fun at whatever mighty power was out there, but to his great relief there was a heartfelt 'amen' from the small congregation.

'Lord, in your mercy, hear our prayer,' Nick added, before he stood up and saw that the mainly elderly and truly religious people who made up the congregation were all nodding or smiling. In fact, there wasn't one wrinkled brow to be seen. But by the time it got to the family service at 11 a.m., Nick knew that the whole village had heard.

For a start the church was fuller than normal. Second, the congregation looked miserable and some had indeed been weeping; others were curious with the round-eyed robin look that hoped they could garner further information. Walking up the centre aisle, the cross being carried before him, Nick decided to cut his sermon, which had been on the subject of spreading joy, and speak instead of the tragedy that had occurred in their midst. Well aware that Patsy Quinn, looking colourful in a violet dress and matching gladiator sandals, was smiling at him, sitting in the third pew from the front, he suddenly realized that Olivia, too, was in church. She was near the back and was quite alone, the dashing inspector no doubt fully occupied with the tragic case. Silently, Nick sighed, thinking what a mixed bag life was – from the genuine happiness of the people who had been at yesterday's Medieval Fair, to the lonely and terrifying death of a small boy in the dark hours after midnight. He found that he was silently asking the question, who could have committed such a gross misdeed against such a tiny, quivering member of the human race?

Hugh Wyatt sat late in his kitchen that night, staring into the depths of a glass of Scotch but not drinking from it, a little habit he had grown into whilst serving in – and surviving – Afghanistan. On the floor, dopey in its cat basket, was the feline Samba, a bandage round the stump of what had once been its tail. Hugh lowered a long finger into the basket and gave the cat an affectionate tickle on the head. Despite his somewhat stoical exterior he was warm-hearted and affectionate and felt that he was being physically racked – that ancient form of torture so beloved of the Tudors – whenever he saw one of his beautiful soldiers maimed beyond human recognition. Hugh was quite straight sexually but to him there was beauty in all forms of human life, and he loathed to see any work of nature hurt or destroyed. Thus, even the attack on his cat – which surely could not have been an accident – had hurt him to the heart.

He was too sensitive for army life but had joined the ranks and gone to Sandhurst to please his father – and grandfather – who had both been high-ranking professional soldiers. And once in, he had accepted it and done the best he could. Yet, though he had strictly abided by the code of conduct, doing his duty and being popular with the men, his heart had been elsewhere, deep in the heart of the countryside, mucking around in his garden and keeping pets.

At last Hugh reached for his glass of Scotch and sipped slowly. The fire was burning low and as a log slipped, making a gentle spluttering sound, there was a creak on the stairs. Instantly Hugh was wide awake, his hand instinctively reaching for the poker. He crept to the kitchen door and opened it silently and infinitesimally, putting his eye to the crack.

Isabelle was creeping down the stairs and just for a second Hugh watched her. She had a jumper on over her pyjama top, though her feet were completely bare, not even slippers on. He wondered what plan she had in her little head.

'Hello, Windflower. Where are you going?'

She gave a violent start and burst into tears immediately. 'Oh, Daddy, I was going to check that Samba was still in his basket. That he hadn't wandered outside again.'

He picked her up and carried her into the kitchen. 'No, darling, he's safe in his basket. Look, there he is. Fast asleep.'

She wept violently into his shirt. 'Oh, Daddy, thank goodness. Promise me that you will look after him.'

'You know I will, darling. I'll look after you all.' Had she heard about the murder, he wondered, and quickly ran through her movements this day. She had been out to play with her friends Debbie and Johnnie, son and daughter of an extremely wealthy family who, frankly, Hugh didn't like at all.

'Did you have a good time when you were out?'

'Not really.'

'Oh, why was that?'

'Because Debbie had heard her mother talking on the phone

and she said that a little boy was shot with an arrow. Daddy, who were they talking about?'

A savage chasm yawned at Hugh's feet. Should he tell his ten-year-old granddaughter and lead her one step further into the harsh realities of brutal life? But he couldn't protect her forever.

'It was Billy,' he said. 'Your school friend.'

Sitting on his knee as she was, she turned her eyes up to him. He would never forget that look, so innocent, so innocuous, yet with all the knowledge of the world deep down in the depths.

'Oh, no,' she cried and started to weep once more.

Hugh suddenly longed for a Scotch and holding tightly to Belle, he leaned to the kitchen table and poured himself another small shot.

'I think it was somebody who likes killing,' she said wisely.

'Why do you say that?'

'Because it was a person who enjoys watching things die.'

'Oh, Belle, that is not a very nice thing to say.'

Intellectually, Hugh agreed with her but he did not like to hear it coming from the mouth of somebody so young.

'I think we should talk about something else, Windflower.'

'Why?'

'Because we should.'

'I think it's a witch, don't you, Daddy?'

'Like a Disney character, with warts and a long nose?'

Belle considered. 'No, I think she is probably young and beautiful and deceives people.'

Hugh smiled to himself. 'You've been reading too many fairy stories. Come on, little one, back to bed with you.'

'Suppose she comes in the night to get us.'

'Don't worry, darling. I'll send her flying.'

But though he had tucked Belle in with many reassurances, Hugh went round the house and checked that everything was locked up tightly before he retired for the night.

TWELVE

Patsy Quinn was a girl full of surprises, for she exhibited a very serious side to her nature when she was interviewed by Inspector Tennant at the vicarage. He and Potter were making it the last call of the day before returning to their respective homes on Sunday evening.

Nick had conducted a thoughtful evensong which Patsy – looking stunning in a red maxi dress – had attended, drawing many inquisitive eyes towards her. Afterwards they had walked back to the vicarage, causing an even greater sensation, and were just settling down for a drink or two and a jolly chit-chat when the knocker on the front door had gone. Nick had inwardly cursed but had gone to answer it in his usual cheery manner.

'Good evening, Vicar. Sorry this is such a late hour to call but we wondered if we could have a brief word with you.'

'Inspector Tennant – or may I call you Dominic after all this time? Do come in. I have a friend here but you don't mind that?'

The inspector hesitated in the doorway. 'I apologize if this is inconvenient. We can always come back another time.'

'No, no, not at all. Please come in.'

They walked into the living room and Sergeant Potter's eyes nearly fell out of his head to see Patsy Quinn of *Britain's Got Stars* fame, sitting on the sofa with her feet tucked under her, neat as you please. She smiled at him and said, 'Good evening.' He made a noise as if something were stuck in his throat.

'Is it too late to offer you a drink?' said Nick hospitably.

'I'll have one but Mark has reached his limit, I'm afraid.'

'Oh, well. Are you staying locally?'

'Yes,' Tennant replied, and did not elaborate.

'I suppose you've come to see me about that horrible business at the fair?'

'Yes, you're right. I'm afraid I'll have to ask you both to account for your movements last night.' A humorous smile twitched at Tennant's lips and he added, 'Unfortunate phraseology, that.'

Miss Quinn burst into a rumbustious laugh and the vicar's face went slightly red. Tennant thought that he had hit on something and felt sorry for Nick. Potter just grinned.

'Miss Quinn, if you would like to go first.'

'Certainly. I came to Lakehurst to open the Medieval Fair because my grandmother comes from the village and I came fifth in a contest on television. Can't think why. Could have been because the other singers were so hopeless. Anyway, my granny is Mrs Platt and she lives in the High Street in Yeoman's Cottage. I spent the night with her and had breakfast with her. That's all I've got to say really, except that the vicar and I are new friends and I spent last evening with him in the Great House.'

'Thank you, Miss Quinn. Do you often come to the village?'

'Not very. I don't visit Granny nearly enough. But I'm on tour most of the time. Not very grand, I'm afraid. Places like The Co-op Club in Salford.'

'I see,' Tennant answered gravely, though he was longing to laugh and enjoy the company and not be on duty.

Potter, who had not taken his eyes off Patsy since he had entered the room, asked, 'Don't you ever come locally to sing?'

'Yes. I do gigs in Hastings and Lewes.'

'What about Eastbourne?'

'Only in the folk club.'

Tennant cleared his throat. 'This is only a formality, Nick, but can you account for yourself last night?'

'Well, I walked Miss Quinn back to Yeoman's, then I came home, watched a bit of TV, then went to bed. I didn't hear about the murder till this morning. The congregation were buzzing with it, even at the early service.'

Tennant nodded. 'I can tell you it was the most gruesome sight I have ever seen, and I've witnessed a few, believe me. Whoever did it is very, very sick.'

'I can't quite imagine it. Was the poor little boy tied to the maypole?'

'In a way. There must have been several people in on it because they had danced around with ribbons and bound him to the maypole with those. It looked like a small, colourful chrysalis.'

'You've spoken to the team we employed, Mr Grimm's Men?'

'Yes. Not all of them, but the leader. A very strange fellow with platinum blond hair. A bit of a devil, I thought.'

'You're probably right,' said Nick seriously. 'Mr Grimm is a Sussex term for Old Nick, you know.'

'I didn't realize that. Thanks for the information. He had such strange eyes.'

'Sounds like *Rosemary's Baby*,' Patsy put in.

'You're too young to have seen that, surely.'

'Nonsense. My grandmother has a DVD of it. Scares me stiff.'

It was at that moment, quite nonsensically, that Nick decided he really liked Patsy Quinn.

'I'm going away tomorrow,' she said to Inspector Tennant. 'Unless you instruct me to do otherwise,' she added with a cheeky grin.

'As long as you can give the sergeant a list of your forwarding addresses.'

'I hope you said that with a smile,' she answered.

'I never smile,' he replied with just the merest flutter of a wink.

Daft Dickie Donkin had wandered his way into Speckled Wood, feeling down in spirits – of both kinds. No alcohol had passed his lips since lunchtime when the landlord of The White Hart had brought him a pint of cider, provided he sat outside on the benches. He – the landlord – had been particularly morose, and Dickie knew the reason why. A little boy, a small innocent, had been inside that cocoon and someone had killed him with an arrow. Had ended that blameless life for no reason that the tramp could possibly think of. He wanted to sing a song to the poor spirit just in case it was hovering near and started very quietly, gathering sound as he went along.

> *Oranges and lemons,*
> *Say the bells of St Clement's.*
> *You owe me five farthings,*
> *Say the bells of St Martin's.*
> *When will you pay me?*
> *Say the bells of Old Bailey.*
> *When I grow rich,*
> *Say the bells of Shoreditch.*

When will that be?
Say the bells of Stepney.
I do not know,
Says the great bell of Bow.
Here comes a candle to light you to bed,
And here comes a chopper to chop off your head!

Not realizing that one or two people were now staring at him, Dickie thought to himself that a chopper had come to chop off that poor child's head, except that it had been an arrow in reality. And then reality slipped and he sat quite still while a tiny cinema played a film in his brain. He saw the whole murder, exactly how it was done and who did it. The only thing was he couldn't identify the people because they were all as small as ants in his mental picture. Everything was reduced to an eighth of its normal size.

'Are you all right?' asked a female voice.

Dickie came back to reality slowly but said nothing.

'I said are you all right? Can I get you anything?'

Dickie pulled at his grizzled forelock, as he'd been trained to do years ago, when memories had been sweet and his grandmother had sung. Slowly he nodded his head.

'Yus, please,' came from his tongue, softly and haltingly.

'What would you like?' The little nurse's face was kindly and round.

Dickie pointed at his empty cider glass and nodded his head.

'Oh, really!' said the little woman. 'I meant an aspirin or something.'

Dickie laughed and turned the nod into a shake. 'No, thank 'ee.'

She walked away and Daft Dickie Donkin was seized with a laughing fit until a couple of gigantic men came and threw him out by the scruff of his neck. Dickie straightened what was left of his old jacket and marched down the lane with dignity. He had no idea where he was going but preferred it to being manhandled by two big louts.

Evening was coming and the shadow of the trees hung over the pathway like ghostly fingers. Dickie began to think of where he would spend the night. Outdoors didn't seem quite so appealing with a murderer wandering on the loose. In Dickie's mind rose a picture of a nice, comfortable barn, filled with sweet-smelling hay and he set up the hill towards Speckled Wood, where there were the riding stables and a sheep farm. And other pleasant places that might offer him a night's hospitality. But the sound of a car approaching made him leap back amongst the trees to where he could watch unseen.

There was a small cottage nestling in a pretty garden and it occurred to Dickie dimly that it must have the most beautiful views which swept down over the countryside to where, surely, there was a glimpse of the sea. It also occurred to him that it might have a tool shed just big enough for a man to get a good night's kip in. But that idea was put on hold as two men got out of the car which pulled up outside.

'Are you going to stay here during the investigation, sir?'

Tennant shook his head. 'Only sometimes. But it's a bit easier now that we've got an incident room in the school. Anyway, can you pick me up in the morning? Eight thirty?'

'I might be a few minutes late.'

'Don't worry. I'll be ready when you arrive.'

'Goodnight, sir.' Potter paused, his hand on the door. 'I'm glad you've found somebody as nice as Olivia.'

'Fingers crossed,' answered Tennant, and knocked gently on the front door.

Dickie watched him go inside and the car drive away, then he stood quietly, trying to concentrate. He had been afraid of policemen for what seemed like most of his life. They had handled him a bit roughly during that other business, which now came back into his mind with great clarity. He had enjoyed doing it, cutting his stepfather's throat from ear to ear. But he could never hurt anyone else, particularly not a small child. The thought brought tears to his eyes and he stood silently weeping, standing alone in the fading light. Then he heard footsteps behind him and, wheeling round, saw a farmer approaching, a broken gun over his arm, a jolly spaniel walking beside him.

'Evening,' said the farmer, and continued on his way, walking right past Dickie, the very picture of nonchalance.

The tramp suddenly needed to make contact, to be with another human being on this first night after that terrible murder.

'Guv,' he called out.

The other turned, held out his hand. 'Giles Fielding,' he said, his Sussex accent light and pleasing to the ear. 'I know who you are,' he continued. 'Seen you around for years. You're Dickie Donkin, aren't you? My gran used to know yours.'

Tears coursed down Daft Dickie's weather-beaten cheeks at the mention of his grandmother.

'Come on now, don't take on. I know there are some nasty people about, what with that murder down at the fair and all. But you can sleep in one of my sheds tonight if that would make you feel any better.'

Dickie nodded enthusiastically and walked along in silence, still weeping.

'Now stop that crying. I've got some nice beer on the go and if you can dry up I'll give you a glass. How would that be?'

Dickie nodded again and loped along beside Giles's sauntering gait, making their way up to the top of the hill where Giles's sheep farm was situated, close to the riding stables once owned by the late Cheryl Hamilton-Harty and now inherited by a second cousin who had turned the place into a proper business-like establishment. And where, sometimes in the very early morning, Giles would sense the presence of her dead husband, the German aristocrat, Michael Mauser.

Night fell over the village of Lakehurst and its neighbouring fields. During the previous hours of darkness some evil soul had forced Billy Needham to stand in front of the maypole on a box – or something similar – and had deliberately taken aim at him and killed him with an arrow. Then the murderer and his or her acolyte had danced round and round the body until it had been entirely covered by the gaudy ribbons which celebrated the merry month of May. It had been a most cruel and sadistic crime, one which one could hardly bear to think about. Yet that was precisely what many of the inhabitants were doing. Inspector Tennant, sleeping happily beside that great violinist, Olivia Beauchamp, woke and gazed at the ceiling and started to think of the horror he had witnessed that day. The Reverend Nicholas Lawrence, awoken by his dear old ghost, William, lay wide-eyed and thought about the general goodness of people brought together by grief.

Major Hugh Wyatt was asleep but dreaming of the horrors of war and seeing men blown to smithereens in front of him. And mothers and fathers throughout Lakehurst smiled at their children and locked up their premises with extra care.

But one evil soul was lying awake and grinning in the darkness, thinking of the pleasure it had experienced in watching the boy die and planning how, soon, it must repeat the performance. Yet not before the heat had died down, not until the police were bored with the case and had pushed off back to Lewes. Then it would be safe to creep out in the moonlight and search for another innocent victim and have fun all over again.

THIRTEEN

The school reopened on Monday morning, aware that one of their classrooms was now out of bounds and instead occupied by a dozen computers and a squad of policemen and women. This was an inconvenience to the teachers and a source of magnificent fun to the children, who tiptoed along the corridor and peeped in through the door's glass windows at the activity inside.

Particularly enjoying this form of recreation were Belle and her cohorts, Debbie and Johnnie. The fourth member of their gang, Billy Needham, was no longer with them, and Debbie was still red round the eyes from crying in bed last night.

'It's no good weeping for him,' said Belle, adopting a somewhat saintly expression. 'My mother says he's gone to a better place.'

'But what he had to suffer in order to go there,' remarked Johnnie, who was aged ten and felt superior to girls.

'He probably enjoyed it,' Belle answered carelessly. 'Come on, the bell is going in a minute. Let's go and pull faces at the policemen.'

'Well, I don't want to,' Debbie said. 'I'm going back to our classroom.'

'Oh, do as you please,' Belle answered, and flounced off in the direction of the incident room.

But her plans were thwarted by the arrival of Tennant and Potter at precisely the moment she and Johnnie crouched down outside the door, their faces peeping over the bottom of the glass.

Tennant had had a great deal of experience with juvenile delinquents which had soured his opinion of the young, even one as entrancing as Belle.

'You're not going to be able to see much from down there,' he commented to the two squatting forms. 'And I am most certainly not going to ask you in. So if I were you I'd get to my lesson in double-quick time.'

Both children were startled and leapt to their feet. Just for a minute Belle and the inspector eyed one another up, his gaze penetrating, hers undergoing a rapid change. She dropped a small curtsey, something which she had discovered won an adult's heart immediately. The man did not seem impressed.

'Shoo,' he said. 'Be off.'

'Kindly go away,' said Potter. 'This is a very serious case regarding one of your schoolmates and we don't need little children pulling faces at the door.'

Johnnie took to his heels but Belle loitered. She dropped another very small curtsey and said, 'I'm so sorry, sir. We won't let it happen again.'

Tennant watched her departing back and said, 'Precocious little madam.'

Mark chuckled. 'When you said "Be Off", I wondered what the B stood for.'

'Not hard to work out,' Tennant answered, and began that morning's briefing.

Meanwhile, in Foxfield, Chris O'Hare was at his day job, owning and running a small car repair shop. He liked working with his hands, enjoyed the challenge of keeping some of the terrible old rust-buckets that he had to service, on the road. It was a special joy when somebody with a wad of cash brought in a decent vehicle for him to look over, and today he was in luck. The retired major from Lakehurst brought in an Alfa Romeo Giulietta for a full service.

'How long do you think you'll be?'

'Should be ready by this evening, sir. It's one that needs to be treated with love, you know. Can't be done in a hurry.'

'I'm afraid the interior is in a bit of a mess. The cat had an accident and we had to take it to the vet. I'm sorry, but the poor thing bled a bit.'

'Oh, I'll clear that up, Major. Have it like a new pin.'

'Reg,' Chris called out as soon as the major had been driven away by his wife in her little runaround, 'I've got a job for you.'

The smallest of the archery team, a short, leathery, cheerful-looking man came on to the forecourt, wiping his hands on a filthy rag.

'And what might that be?'

'The major's cat bled all over his car. Would you be kind enough to clean it up?'

'You always keep the dirty jobs for me.'

'That's because you're so easy-going, Reg. You'd do anything for anyone, you would.'

Reg laughed and winked a vivid brown eye. He looked like a garden gnome with the paint peeling off. He had shaved his head and had his chest waxed. In fact, the only hair on him was pubic and that, according to local legend, was massive. As were his feats with the ladies, which were monumental, according to him, legend being quiet on that point.

Reg sighed, hitched up his brown dungarees and was making his way back into the workroom when Chris suddenly called out 'Coppers' and a second later an official car slid into their line of vision.

'What do the bastards want now?' said Chris under his breath.

But Reg had no time to answer as the door opened and out of the car got Sergeant Potter and Inspector Dominic Tennant, looking tremendously attractive and not at all what Reg would have considered to be the kind of copper he was used to.

'Good morning', said Dominic and produced his identification.

'Do you wish to speak to me or Mr Marney or both of us?' asked Chris, his hair almost white in the early sun.

Potter answered. 'Mr Marney actually. We've just come from your house where we were directed on to here.'

Reg grinned and Tennant thought that there was absolutely nothing more lascivious than a bald gnome looking pleased with himself.

'That would be Donna-Marie,' Reg said, and winked one of his dark brown orbs at Potter.

'Really?' said Tennant, and then, because he couldn't resist it, said, 'Your daughter?'

The bald gnome grinned – he had very small teeth with a couple of gold ones in the top – and said, 'No, me girlfriend. What did you think of her?'

'I couldn't really say,' Potter answered. 'She told us where you worked and then rushed out of the house. Said she was late.'

Marney opened his mouth to continue talking about his love life but Tennant cut him short.

'Mr Marney, I would like to ask if you can tell us exactly what you did after the end of the fair. In other words, where were you exactly and what did you do?'

The gnome scratched his bald pate with a leathery hand. 'Well, let me see now. When the fair closed I packed up my equipment.' He gave a dirty laugh which both Tennant and Potter ignored. 'Then went off with the other blokes to The White Hart. No, that's not quite true. I spent a few minutes talking to a group of young ladies who had come up to see my longbow, which is very special, I can tell you.'

The two policemen studiously ignored the double entendre and continued to listen.

'Well, one of them asked me to show her the woods and we went into them for about half an hour.'

'Can you tell me the name of this person, please?'

'It was Lois. That's all I know. I think she lives in Lakehurst but I'm not sure.'

Potter, who was writing madly in his notebook, looked up. 'Did you see anybody else while you were there?'

'Only that mad old tramp who hangs around. Daft Dickie they call him.'

'What was he doing?'

'Watching us. We were having a quickie and I was going at it—'

'Thank you,' interrupted Tennant.

'Well, I shouted at him and he ran off. He's a crazy old bugger but he's quite harmless.'

'What's his real name?'

'Richard Donkin, I imagine. Don't really know because he's been called Dickie as long as I can remember.'

'And what happened when you had finished in the woods?'

'I popped into the Great House but then me and the other archers went off to our local in Foxfield.'

'That's the haunt of the morris men, isn't it?'

'Yes, most of them were in there but not my boss Chris. I left him in the Great House making a great effort with a girl, who was very cut-glass. I don't think he was getting very far.'

Tennant nodded. 'And were you at home alone that night?'

Reg Marney looked slightly shamefaced. 'Yes, I was, truth to tell.'

'Did you know the murdered boy?'

'No, never met him. Poor little sod.'

They stood up, making their way out of the dingy office into which they had been shown. Chris O'Hare was under the bonnet of a car but looked up as the two policemen walked past.

'Have you heard from Skye at all?' asked Tennant casually.

'Not a dicky bird. I tell you, Inspector, there was something odd about that girl.'

'Can you be a little more exact?'

'Well she insisted that we sit round the corner of the pub, as if she was trying to keep her presence hidden from the crowd. Not that she need have worried with that silly Patsy Quinn bitch there signing autographs. Can't think how she got a career going when she only came fifth.'

'I think she's jolly good,' said Potter. 'She's got a nice personality, which is more than you can say for some of the terrible people who win.'

Tennant said reprovingly, 'We're here to discuss a brutal murder, not pop stars. Go on about Skye, Mr O'Hare.'

Chris straightened up and said, 'If I want her I could get her, you know.'

'You'd use witchcraft I suppose,' said Potter acidly, still slightly annoyed by Tennant's last remark.

The car mechanic slanted his eyes. 'Is that what you think?'

'Yes, I do. Would you?'

'I'd rather not discuss it. It weakens the spell. Let's simply say that there are cunning tricks as old as time itself that one can use to bring a lady to your side.'

Tennant would rather have died than admit it but he felt a thrill of interest, which he firmly clamped down.

'Mr O'Hare, is there anything further you want to tell me about Skye?'

'I've told you already. She had an upper-class accent and had obviously been to a good school. She said she wanted to walk home and I said I would walk with her. But she insisted that I leave her at a certain point. I tried to kiss her but she pushed me away and said my black make-up would spoil her dress. That's all that happened and that's all I have to say. We made no arrangements to meet again.'

'Thank you very much. We'll let you know if we hear any more of her,' said Potter.

Afterwards in the car Tennant said, 'Why did you say that? We're not running a dating service.'

'Sorry, sir. I can't seem to do a thing right today.'

There was silence for a few moments then Tennant said, 'Let's go to the incident room. I could do with an hour or two on the computer.'

As they turned into Lakehurst High Street they saw Patsy Quinn leave her grandmother's house, get into her small blue car and head off in the direction of London.

'One unhappy little vicar, I believe' said Tennant, and Potter, his humour restored, nodded his head and gave an answering grin.

In the vicarage Nick was having a brief break before he got into his car and started on the duty of taking communion to the bedbound. It was something that often brought him much joy but today his mind was full of Patsy Quinn and the feeling that this was a relationship he was going to pursue to the limit – whatever that turned out to be. In the last two days he had seen as much of her as was decently possible and, despite the fact that a shadow had been cast over everyone by the savage killing of a blameless boy, he had enjoyed his time spent in her company. She was attractive – bordering on beautiful – but it was her extraordinary golden glow that had captivated his heart.

Nick sat very still, his mug of lapsang souchong halfway to his lips, wondering at the fact that he had used that phrase, even privately, to himself. It was delightfully old-fashioned but it summed up exactly what his feelings were. He was falling in love, and instantly following this revelation came the horrid thought that he was not certain how to proceed. The best way might be through her grandmother, he thought, and made a mental note to visit Mrs Platt quite shortly.

There being only two bedridden people to call on, so frail that he had to lift their heads to receive the Holy Sacrament, Nick decided to look up his friends at Fulke Castle when the short services were finished. He had always loved the place, even though the very sight of it overawed him. And today was no different. It reared up out of its moat, the ancient bricks telling the story of its incredible past, a past which the vicar knew well, having participated in a Son et Lumière held within its ancient walls. Having rung Sir Rufus to check that it was convenient, Nick drove across the causeway and parked his car in the private car park.

Rufus opened the door into the Victorian part, his hair the colour of beaten copper in the sunshine.

'Nick, do come in. As I told you, the girls are all out so it's just me, I'm afraid.'

'I won't stay long, if you don't mind. I just called to see if the bad news had reached your ears.'

'You mean about the killing of that small boy? Oh, yes, we heard it on Sunday. One of the kitchen staff came in and told the rest and it soon came round to our part of the castle. Is it true he was shot by an arrow?' Nick nodded. 'It must have been some lunatic. Nobody in their right mind would contemplate such a thing.'

'Our old friend Inspector Tennant is in charge of the case.'

'Is he? Well, that's one good thing, I suppose. The news quite upset the girls, particularly Araminta. She burst into tears.'

'How old is she now?'

'Just eighteen. The phone never stops ringing. All would-be boyfriends.'

'Does she have anyone in particular?'

'She's got a crush on one of the younger brothers of a friend of mine. It's all rather alarming.'

'How old is he, for heaven's sake?'

'Twenty-eight. And he's been married and divorced.'

Nick sighed. 'I'm afraid we must move with the times, Sir Rufus.'

'I thought I did until it came to my own wretched daughter. Do you think it is too early for a drink?'

Nick looked at his watch. 'I think it is.'

Rufus laughed. 'I take it that's a yes.'

Nick answered. 'A very weak one. I'm driving.'

Rufus looked at him and shook his head. 'I'm hardly likely to ring the police, now am I?'

The vicar could think of no suitable reply.

In the somewhat cramped conditions of one of the school's classrooms, Potter looked across at Tennant and shouted, 'Sir.'

'Yes?'

'I think I've got something. Listen to this. Richard Donkin was questioned under caution about the murder of his stepfather in 1989 but they couldn't find enough evidence to pin it on him. His stepfather, George Grimes, was apparently extremely violent to both him and his mother and was discovered with his throat slashed from ear to ear, with no sign of forced entry or burglary. They had a ghastly time trying to interview Donkin because he's pretty well autistic.'

'Here, let me have a look at that, will you?'

Potter obligingly slid off the seat and Tennant took his place in front of the computer.

'Well, bugger me,' he said. 'The consensus was that the boy was guilty as hell but they simply hadn't enough evidence to charge him.'

'Apparently some old farmer stuck up for him and wouldn't be shifted from his story. Provided the perfect alibi. Says Donkin slept in his barn and he saw him in there asleep at one o'clock in the morning.'

'I think we should get our Dickie in for questioning. I'll get a psychiatrist who specializes in dealing with autism to come along.'

'I don't know that that will do much good, sir. He might just sit there mute.'

'It's all very well to think about that. We've got to find him first.'

'Very true.'

'I'll ask Lewes to let me have a few extra men.'

'I think we're probably going to need them.'

Dickie had gladly accepted Giles Fielding's offer of an early evening meal. It had been some while since he had eaten anything hot and cooked – if one discounted the odd burger – and so he sat in appreciative silence while his host poured him a jug of beer and threw another log on the farmhouse fire.

Opposite Giles's house and sheep fields was a small lane and the only building in it was Olivia's weekend house, which she had inherited from her parents and which she only came down to late on a Friday evening. Giles kept a weather-beaten eye on it for her, not so much fearing a burglar but lads from the village playing silly buggers, and up till now she had always been glad of his reassuring neighbourly presence. But these days she found that she was spending a little more time there – engagements permitting – and was very much enjoying her new romance with the debonair inspector, so different from anything portrayed on television. In truth, she was more drawn to Dominic Tennant than she would admit even to herself. So it was with a certain lift of her heart that Olivia heard his gentle knock at the door. She flung it open but it was to see a small girl standing there. The child looked absolutely terrified.

'Can you please help me, I'm lost,' she said.

'Good gracious. Come in. What's happened to you?'

'Our mothers took us out for a picnic but I ran away and now I don't know where I am. Yours was the only light on so I knocked.'

And with that the wretched child burst into a veritable flood of unattractive tears and screwed her face up so that she resembled a small pig in extremis.

Olivia – not used to children – thought wildly and decided to be tough.

'Now do stop crying and tell me where you live. If you give me your phone number I'll ring your parents and then they can come and fetch you.'

The child looked up, her eyes like saucers behind her spectacles.

'I've only got a mummy.'

'Well, give me her number then.'

'Daddy ran off with a tarty blonde,' the girl rambled on, undeterred. 'She was his PA and Mummy said that she was in every sense of the word.'

'Oh dear,' answered Olivia, somewhat nonplussed.

'I've met her,' the monologue continued. 'She's got long fair hair to her shoulders and she flicks her head about every few minutes to move it. Her name is Scarlett. Can I have a biscuit, please?'

'What? Oh, yes.' Olivia dived into the small kitchen and produced a packet of shortbread. The child took one, said, 'Thank you,' and fell silent while she chewed.

'What's your name?'

'Debbie Richards. My Mummy is Mrs Richards.'

'Yes, I gathered that. Now tell me your telephone number like a good girl.'

'I think it's 515677.'

Olivia dialled the number and a voice with a slight Estuary accent answered.

'Mrs Richards?'

'Yes.'

'I've got your little girl here. I'm afraid she got lost but she's perfectly safe. Can you come and fetch her or would you like me to bring her back?'

'I thought she was doing a sleepover at Belle's.'

In desperation Olivia thrust the phone at Debbie and commanded, 'Speak to your mother.'

'Hello, Mummy. I ran away from Belle because she kept telling me ghost stories and I got frightened.'

Olivia could hear the voice at the other end distinctly.

'Why did you do a thing like that? You'll have them all worried sick. Where are you now?'

Olivia mouthed, 'Speckled Wood,' and Debbie repeated it.

'Well, you can jolly well stay there while I phone Mrs Wyatt. Then I'll come for you and you can go straight to bed. You're a very, very naughty girl. Where exactly are you?'

Olivia took the phone from Debbie. 'My name is Olivia Beauchamp and I live at Starlight Cottage, Tinkers Lane, Speckled Wood. Have you got a satnav?'

Of course Mummy had, so the postcode was duly given. Meanwhile Debbie was stolidly eating her way through the short-bread and looking most unattractive with her nose starting to run. Olivia made a silent vow never, but never, to have children.

Eventually Mrs Richards turned up looking frazzled, so much so that the violinist found herself offering the woman a glass of wine.

'Oh, yes, please. It's been ever so kind of you to take her in. I don't know what's got into Debbie recently. I mean Isabelle is her best friend and Debbie is used to her telling stories. Why she should get frightened, I just can't think.'

'Apparently they were ghostly and Debbie panicked. I must admit I don't like the creepy ones much even though they hold a certain fascination.'

'Yes. I don't go for them myself. Prefer romantic trash. I've got a Kindle, have you?'

'No, I prefer the feel of a book.'

In the background they could hear Debbie start to cry again.

'Oh, Mummy, it was so horrible.'

'Yes, Debbie, I'm sure it was. Now shut up and let me finish my wine in peace.'

Half an hour later they were still there and Olivia was wondering how late Dominic was going to be. But eventually a rather pink-cheeked Mrs Richards bundled the pallid Debbie into their car and drove off into the night. Olivia stood on her doorstep and breathed in the beauties of a May evening with the sun just going down behind the stark outline of the Victorian orphanage, now standing empty and spectral against the crimson sky. She was just going back in when she heard a distant voice singing and smiled to herself.

> *Over the quiet hills*
> *Slowly the shadows fall;*
> *Far down the echoing vale*
> *Birds softly call;*
> *Slowly the golden sun*
> *Sinks in the dreaming west;*
> *Bird songs at eventide*
> *Call me, call me to rest.*

Olivia had never heard Giles sing like that, in such a beautiful, light baritone. She leaned her head against the doorpost and felt her heart rate speed up at the sound of a distant car approaching. And suddenly she wanted to play. Dashing into the house she picked up her violin, tucked it beneath her chin and played 'Bird Song at Eventide' to welcome Dominic home.

FOURTEEN

I t should have been a relatively peaceful night. There was a good-sized police presence in Lakehurst and the surrounding area and several plain-clothes officers watching the pubs and being unobtrusive. But for all the reassurance, Nick simply could not get off to sleep. William had been in an agitated mood until eventually the vicar had shouted, 'Shut up, William, or I'll exorcize you.' This had brought peace at last but despite the quiet Nick had still been unable to rest. Was it the beautiful Queen Guinevere – or Patsy Quinn in everyday life – that was unnerving him? But he had spoken to her on the phone that evening and she had promised to come to Lakehurst next weekend so he had been in touch with her, though she had sounded a bit flippant at the other end, he had to admit. Yet the fact was that, despite everything, Nick could not sleep.

He got up, put on his dressing gown and went downstairs to make himself a cup of herbal tea. Then he switched on the television and stared at the screen. It was a horror film, with a frightened girl fleeing through the deserted streets of pre-war Berlin, pursued by something unseen, which threw an enormous shadow before it. Nick watched for a few minutes before saying 'Rubbish' overloudly and switching the film off. He sat, sipping his tea, listening to the silence but not before he had been to the front door and, unlocking it, looked out.

Lakehurst High Street was deserted. Nothing moved, and yet somehow Nick could have sworn that he was not alone, that some other creature was out and about, doing mischief. It was an uncomfortable feeling and eventually, tea drunk and mug washed, Nick took a sleeping pill before returning to his lonely bed, on which, obviously having crept in during his absence, Radetsky now slept.

The first shards of daylight came at about five and every bird in Christendom gave throat, a great hymn to greet the dawn. The

policeman who had taken over the shift guarding the site where
the fair had been held, drew in a breath at the rosiness of it all,
loving the sound that the feathered flock were making and
thinking wryly over the number of times he had cursed them
when they had woken him up at dawning. He started his slow
perambulation round the area, looking carefully for something,
anything in fact, to relieve the slight feeling of tension that had
suddenly gripped him. And then he saw it. In the field beyond
this one, supported by a garden spade, stood a very small scarecrow, a hat pulled down over its eyes, a pair of wellington-booted
feet sticking out, and a trickle of blood drying on the front of
its nightdress. PC Coppice shouted, 'Oh shit,' and started to run
towards it.

It was even worse than it looked from a distance. When he
pulled the hat off he could see that the child's head had been
staved in by a blunt instrument and that she had peed herself
with fright. PC Coppice took a few steps away and threw up
before collecting himself and using his radio to call help.

They were there within minutes and Sergeant Mark Potter,
who had spent the night at the Great House and had risen at
dawn and was showing a night's growth of ebony beard on his
chin, was the first near the corpse.

'Did you touch anything?' he asked Scott Coppice.

'Yes, sir, I pulled off the hat. The face was completely hidden
and I had to have a look.'

Mark nodded. 'No, that's fine. We can identify your prints.
Poor little bugger. What tortured mind could do this to a child?
There must be some sadistic madman on the loose.'

'I've never seen anything like it.'

'How old would you say the child was?'

'About ten. And who could persuade her to come out into the
field at night?'

'If we knew that we'd be halfway to solving the crime.'

In due course and as quickly as they could manage, the rest
of the team appeared. Inspector Tennant looked very slightly
ruffled. He had shaved, but his tie was a little askew and his suit
had obviously been put on in some haste. Potter, glancing at him
surreptitiously, gave a hidden smile. He sincerely wished that
this Olivia affair would resolve into something more permanent.

It was high time his boss settled down again – this time with a happier outcome, let it be hoped.

The doctor looked horror-struck for a moment before putting her professional face on.

'Is this the work of the other killer?' Tennant asked.

'I should think so. This poor child was beaten to death with that spade which is holding her up. I'd say this was the work of a juvenile hater.'

'Agreed. And there's something horribly ritualistic about the two deaths. That wretched little boy being struck by an arrow and now this poor tot made to resemble a scarecrow. Frankly, it's sick.'

Potter met his eye. 'Do you think this could be connected with Mr Grimm, sir?'

'Do you mean the morris dancers or the Devil himself?'

'Possibly both.'

'Let's get Mr O'Hare in for questioning. Oh, and while we're at it, that other archer, Reg Marney.'

'Are you thinking what I'm thinking?'

'Very possibly, yes.'

The doctor, with assistance, lifted the corpse down and the spade was bagged up immediately. Looking at the little girl lying on the ground, Tennant was struck by the pathos of the scene. The doctor had lifted the child's nightdress, displaying that she was naked beneath and that her bare feet had been shoved into the wellies.

'Looks as if she was got out of bed by someone or other,' he remarked.

'It must have been somebody she knew.'

'Or someone she was afraid of.'

'Yes, you're right.'

'This is a deep case, Mark, and I've got a nasty feeling that we've got to solve it quickly.'

'You think the killer might strike again?'

'I feel pretty certain that they will.'

And with those words of warning the inspector left the doctor to continue her work.

Olivia was up and drinking a coffee when there came a loud and persistent knocking on her door. Now what? she thought, and rather reluctantly went to open it.

Mrs Richards was standing there looking like a phantom, her mascara – left over from the night before – streaking her powder white face, her lips pale and bloodless.

Olivia gaped and said, 'Whatever's the matter?'

'It's Debbie,' the woman panted. 'Is she with you?'

'No,' Olivia exclaimed in some surprise. 'I haven't seen her since last night. Why, what's happened?'

'She's not in her bed, she's not in the house, she's not anywhere around. She's run away and I just thought she might have come to you.' She looked piteous. 'May I come in for a moment?'

'But of course,' said Olivia, standing aside. 'Would you like some coffee?'

'Yes, please. I feel wrung out with worry.'

And she leant on the kitchen table and cried as if she would never stop. Olivia poured out a cup and sat down opposite her, wondering what she could do. She had Dominic's mobile number but he had asked please not to ring him unless it were a dire emergency. Looking at the shuddering wreck sitting opposite her, she decided that this was.

He answered crisply, in a professional voice. 'Tennant.'

'I know that you told me not to ring you on this number but something has come up.

It's about that child that called on me last night, Debbie Richards. Her mother's here and the girl has gone missing. I just thought I ought to let you know.'

'Can you describe her, please?'

'She's about ten. Fair hair, blue eyes.'

'Height?' Dominic's voice cut across.

'About three feet, I should imagine. You know, the usual size for kids that age.'

There was a pause at the other end and then Tennant said, 'Olivia, see if you can persuade Mrs Richards to go with you to Lewes.'

'Why?'

'There's a body going to the mortuary there now.'

'Oh, God!' Olivia exclaimed and Mrs Richards looked up.

'Do it if you can, darling. I'll send a police car in the next thirty minutes.' He rang off.

Olivia slipped the mobile into her dressing gown pocket,

thinking that this must be exactly what being a policeman's partner would be like. Could she stand it? Would it fit in with her highly disciplined life as a leading solo violinist? The answer was a slightly edgy yes, provided that the policeman was Dominic Tennant.

Mrs Richard looked at her blearily over the rim of her coffee mug.

'Was that anything important?'

'Yes, I think it was. They want you to go to Lewes.'

'What for?'

'I don't know and that's the honest truth. Maybe Debbie has been taken there.'

Mrs Richards shot to her feet. 'Oh my God, I must go to her now. Is she all right? Did they say?'

'No, not a word. They said they would send a police car and that I was to accompany you.'

The poor woman went completely white, like ivory. 'Why? What for? Do you think it is bad news?'

'I don't know,' Olivia answered desperately. 'But whatever it is, we'll face it together.'

Mrs Richards wept afresh and Olivia took the opportunity of rushing upstairs and hastily getting dressed. By the time she returned the police car was pulling up outside and she helped the trembling woman get in.

To describe the rest of the drive as hellish would not be an exaggeration. Susan Richards collapsed and lay in Olivia's lap, weeping dismally. But when she saw the word 'Mortuary' discreetly hidden in the doorway, she went berserk and a doctor had to be called to give her a calming injection. Dominic finally turned up, and took over the entire situation.

'Mrs Richards, try to be calm. I do realize it is a horrible thing we are asking you to do but be a brave girl.'

'But what is it you want?' she asked, bewildered but calmer as the injection began to take effect.

'I want you to come and identify a body. It is that of a small girl who at the moment is without a name.'

She clutched him by the lapels. 'Is it Debbie?'

'I don't know,' he said.

'Come with me,' she said to Olivia, clutching her hand.

Looking down at the little person, cleaned up, the top of her head hidden, wearing a small white robe that was clearly mortuary property, Olivia felt no sense of shock, for the child merely looked as if she were sleeping. In fact, an enormous sense of peace emanated from her.

Susan Richards said in a very quiet voice, 'Yes, that's my Debbie.'

'I'm going to ask a policewoman to come home with you and stay,' Tennant said quietly. 'It will be company for you in the house and she can help you with all the little chores.' Then he added, 'Did Debbie remain at home last night or did she go on a sleepover?'

'I should say she didn't! I was punishing her for running away. She went straight to bed when we returned home.' Her face became glacial. 'Does that mean that she left the house when it was dark?'

'That, or somebody came and took her.'

'But how could that have happened? I would have heard an intruder.'

Dominic was being ultra gentle. 'Nothing is very clear at the moment. But later today my boys will come and look over your premises and see if anything is revealed. But in the meanwhile, Mrs Richards, I would suggest that you go home with WPC Monica Jones and go straight to bed with a nice hot drink. Nothing can ever express how terrible you must be feeling at the moment but I assure you that in time the pain will ease.'

Olivia looked at him rather helplessly. 'I got a lift in a police car here so I'll need one back. My own car is at home.'

'I'll get one of the PCs to drive you back. Mrs Richards, we'll want to have a good look at your car.'

Oh God, thought Olivia, it could play an important part in the story. Suppose somebody drove poor Debbie to the field last night. She sat down rather suddenly.

'Come back to the station and I'll fix everything up,' he said, and Olivia wished that they were somewhere other than the grimmest place in the world, the city mortuary.

Quarter of an hour later they went off in a little procession, Olivia arriving first because it was the least far to go. But once in her house she paced restlessly, not even able to play her violin, her mind too full of terrible thoughts. In the end she rang the vicar and asked if she could meet him at the Great House.

'I'd be delighted. Olivia, what's wrong? Your voice sounds odd.'

'Then you haven't heard the news. That poor child Debbie Richards was murdered last night, not far from that little boy. Oh God, Nick, I went with her mother this morning and saw her in the mortuary. It was really ghastly.'

'Come out now. I was supposed to meet the churchwarden, but I'll cancel it. I'll see you in half an hour.'

She was leaving the house as Giles came into her line of vision, carrying a lamb under his arm. He looked every inch the countryman, with his leather boots and tweed waistcoat and his sporty cap pulled down over one eye. But he caught her mood with a look and hurried towards her, the lamb wailing like a lost child.

'What's the matter, little angel? What's troubling you?'

It was too much. Olivia collapsed weeping against his comforting chest, the lamb running round his feet. 'There's been another murder,' she gasped.

Giles eased her away and looked aghast. 'Who?'

'Debbie Richards, that little tot who was a friend of Billy's. I saw her last night. She was picnicking in the woods and got lost. She came to my house because the lights were on.'

'My God,' said Giles softly. 'I think it's time for a few vigilantes.'

'Oh, Giles, you wouldn't. I mean it's against the law. And the police are keeping an eye on that area, I can assure you.'

'I'm sure they are. And no disrespect to your boyfriend, but maybe they could do with a little local backup.' He picked the lamb up again. 'Got something stuck in its foot. Limping like a good 'un.'

'Poor thing. Well, I'm off to the Great House to see Nick. He's a good listener when it comes to pouring out your troubles.'

'He is that. I might come down for a lunchtime pint. It all depends on the sheep. Incidentally, don't say a word about my vigilante idea. I've got to consult a few of the lads first.'

'I won't say anything. Thanks for being such a good neighbour.'

'Promised your mum I'd look after you and I never go back on my word.'

By the time Olivia reached the village, the word was out. People were standing in small clusters in the High Street discussing the terrible facts and looking very pale about the gills. Others – the majority – had packed the Great House, despite the fact that it was barely lunchtime, and fortifying themselves. Jack Boggis sat in his usual chair, fulminating.

'I think it's time that they reintroduced capital punishment. That's what I'd do to bastards like child killers. I'd hang, draw and quarter 'em in full public spectacle.' He drew deeply on his tankard and looked round to see who was agreeing with him. Nobody was, in fact no one was even speaking to him. Nonetheless he continued at full spate. 'I ask you, what normal man would go round molesting little children and then killing 'em, that's what I want to know. And it's no good looking at me like that, young man. I was out in the desert, let me tell you, and I know a thing or two – and I've seen a thing or two as well.' He drained his tankard and set off in a rather wobbly direction for the bar.

Olivia, following him with her eyes, said, 'He's truly pathetic, that man.'

Nick answered, 'I know. But don't let him hear you say that. He thinks he's cock-of-the-walk.'

'Why does that always sound vaguely obscene?'

Nick grinned and said, 'It's good that you can still smile.'

'I don't know how I've got the face to do it after what I've been through in the last twenty-four hours.'

'That's what makes us human, God be thanked. If every shock and every blow and every disappointment we had ever had removed our ability to smile, then we would turn into a race of ghastly, gloomy gnomes that would plod round the earth in misery.'

Despite everything, Olivia grinned. 'You vicars have a way with words,' she said.

'Happen,' said Jack Boggis to no one at all as absolutely nobody was listening.

Much later that evening after Tennant had spent hours at the incident room briefing the house-to-house brigade, doubling

the strength of the patrol round the fields and calling in Mr
O'Hare, who said he couldn't make it till seven o'clock, Dominic
went to see Susan Richards. He had first telephoned the WPC
and asked the situation. He had been told that Mrs Richards had
been forced to calm herself as her younger child, Jonathan, needed
attention. She was currently making him boiled egg and soldiers
for his supper. Tennant had nodded, satisfied, phoned Olivia to
warn her that he was going to be late and had gone for a quick
hike round the fields in order to see for himself the amount of
cover they had.

It struck him forcibly, walking round the perimeter, what a
fickle creature nature was. Now, standing in the blessed light of
a May sunset, with birds calling from the trees, pink and white
blossom smothering the branches like a bride's veils, the air so
clear that one could see a leaf drop a mile away, Dominic thought
back to the field's recent history. On Saturday it had been the
scene of an historic event, with people dressing up and taking
part enthusiastically. Arrows had shot through the air, morris
dancers had leapt as one, beautiful maidens had been pursued
by the grinning wicked hobby horse. And then douse the candles,
put out the lights, and wickedness had crept out of the darkness
and killed an innocent little boy. The next night, the same thing.
A small girl had been dressed as a scarecrow and her poor wispy
head had been bludgeoned in with a spade. And now the hours
of darkness were coming once more.

He spoke to Potter on his mobile. 'Mark, go and see the leader
of that longbow team. Get his view on the entry point of the
arrow. Take some photographs with you. He will probably be in
by now. His address is on the file.'

'You mean the man from The Closed Loop?'

'I think they all belong to that but the one that seemed to be
in charge, yes.'

'I'm on my way, as they say in Star Trek.'

'Thunderbirds Are Go.'

'Blimey, that dates you, sir.'

'Oh, God,' the inspector answered, and rang off.

It was time to end his evening sojourn and go to see the
stricken Mrs Richards. WPC Monica Jones – one of the most
caring and finest at dealing with this sort of situation – had

obviously worked her own particular magic because the house was quiet when he rang the bell. Eventually the policewoman answered it after the brief sound of someone going upstairs.

'She's taking Johnnie up to bed and I've promised to read him a story so that she can speak to you.'

'How is she?'

'Stricken to the heart. She blames herself for some reason.'

'What about the husband?'

'Traded her in for a younger model.'

'I suppose he's in the Algarve.'

'Got it in one. He's been telephoned and he's flying back overnight. Should be around tomorrow.'

The inspector sighed heavily and at that moment Susan came down the stairs.

'Hello, Inspector. Go into the sitting room, will you.'

He did so and she followed him in, saying, 'Do take a seat. Would you like anything? A cup of coffee?'

'No, thanks. I just hope that you can bear to tell me the story of exactly what happened yesterday evening and night.'

'I'll try to. I'm not lying if I say the wrong thing. It's just that I'm trying to get it straight in my mind.' Tennant nodded. 'Well, it's school holidays as you know and that means that Debbie spends a lot of time playing with her friends. Johnnie joins them sometimes. But not all the time. Anyway, on this occasion he stayed with me and had a friend over to tea. Debbie had gone to Belle's house for a picnic, to be followed by a sleepover. It seems they went off to Speckled Wood, which is quite pleasant I believe. I don't know if Belle's grandmother – she calls her Mummy because it is the only one she has known – went to sleep or what but the two girls wandered off and, according to Debbie, Belle began to tell her the grimmest kind of ghost story, saying the woods were haunted and that there was something like a Blair Witch figure living in them and if she saw them she would kill Debbie. Anyway the poor child was so scared that she ran away and knocked on the door of the only house she could see. It was owned by quite a famous woman, Olivia Beauchamp, some kind of violinist. Do you know her?'

'Oh yes, we've met,' Tennant answered, straight-faced.

'Well, she phoned me and I went to get Debbie straight away.'

'Go on.'

'I told her that she mustn't listen to silly stories that Belle told her and that if she went on like that I wouldn't let Debbie play with her any more.'

She paused, her face flushed and mottled. 'Would you mind if I had a drink?' she asked. 'Can I tempt you to one?'

'Unfortunately not. I'm still on duty, I'm afraid.'

She went to the sideboard and poured herself a treble gin and tonic, then took a seat. She had started to cry again.

'It's just the pity of it all,' she said. 'Her little dead face looked as if she were only asleep, not finished.'

'Can't you try and think of her like that?' Tennant said quietly.

'No,' she screamed at him, 'no, no, no. That was my child, the creature that started in my womb and which I brought silently into the world. It was such a quiet moment, you see. "One last push" said the midwife and I gave one and I felt her slither out. There was total silence for a moment and then someone said "Give her to me" and I heard them smack her – yes, they smacked her bottom – to make her take that first, vital breath. And now what is it for? She has been snuffed out and there is nothing anyone can do or say ever that will take away the hurt.'

Tennant sat very still, not knowing how to deal with her, wishing that he had a child so that he could know something of the pain she was feeling. Instead he just put out his hand and covered hers, trying to take some of the suffering away from her. She looked at him, her face barely recognizable, so twisted was it with hurt.

'Thank you,' she whispered. 'You are very kind.'

At that moment WPC Jones came through the door and took in the situation with a glance. 'There, there,' she said, going to Susan and kneeling by her. 'Don't cry, my love. The inspector has to ask you a few questions just so that we can find this monster and put him away forever.'

Susan blew her nose with vigour. 'Yes, you're right.' She gulped down the gin in one go and said, 'Can you give me a refill, please.' Then she turned her poor face to Dominic and said, 'Sorry, Inspector.'

'So, Debbie slept at home last night.'

'Yes.'

'And she didn't go out at all that you knew of?'

'No. I went to bed early and read for quite a long while. I heard somebody go to the lavatory – either Debbie or Johnnie – but I didn't call out. After that, I slept like a log till this morning.'

'When you presumably put your head round the door and discovered her gone?'

'I looked all over the house and found the back door closed but unlocked.'

'You won't mind if the forensic team move in for a day or two?'

'Must they? Why?'

'There may be vital clues as to where she went.'

'Or even if somebody came and snatched her,' put in Monica Jones.

'But I would have heard them, surely.'

'Not necessarily,' the policewoman answered, and her eyes flicked briefly over the gin bottle.

Tennant's mind was racing ahead. By this late stage, particularly with an active small boy and a frantic mother in the house, most of the evidence would be badly corrupted. But it would be worth a try. Yet who could have crept in so silently and summoned Debbie from her bed? Probably nobody. He imagined that someone threw a pebble at her window until she woke up and looked out. So she must have known her attacker. But that threw the field wide open, from great friend to casual acquaintance. Yet whoever it was must have offered some attraction for the child to go out, her feet thrust into wellingtons, nothing on beneath her nightdress. He stood up.

'Mrs Richards, you have been most kind and tolerant to allow me in at such a difficult time. I would suggest that you and Johnnie go away for a couple of days while forensics look at your house. That is, if you would like that.'

'No, I wouldn't,' she said. 'I want to be around when they turn my house upside down.'

'As you wish, of course. Goodnight, Mrs Richards. Try and get to bed early.'

'There'll be no rest for me tonight. If I go to sleep I might have bad dreams.'

In the hallway he muttered to WPC Jones, 'For God's sake keep an eye on her. She looks fit to do anything.'

'I will, sir, don't you worry. I'll sleep at the foot of her bed, if necessary.'

'As if she were Queen Elizabeth I?'

'Just as if.'

'Chamber pot and all?'

'Well, one must draw the line somewhere,' answered Monica Jones and smiled quietly.

FIFTEEN

Potter was having a most peculiar time with Nigel Cuthbert-Campbell, who – or so it seemed to the sergeant – dwelled entirely in the past. By day he worked for the council in some capacity or other, but by night, and most definitely at weekends, he buckled his sword at his side, metaphorically speaking, and became Sir Nigel, ruled by strict obedience to the laws of chivalry.

He answered the door to Potter's knock dressed in a pair of tights which left nothing to the imagination, and an emerald green tunic. Like it or not, Potter's eyes were drawn immediately to the man's crotch, which seemed extremely padded out.

'Come in,' said Nigel in a voice which should have been fulsome and round but which, instead, was very slightly whiny. 'And what may I do for you, good sir?'

Potter showed his badge at which Nigel's face underwent a slight transformation, from merry rat to bad-tempered rodent.

'What's it about?' he said.

'I'm sorry to have to inform you, sir, that there has been a second murder and we are questioning everybody who took part in the Medieval Fair the other day.'

'A second murder, you say? Who was the victim?'

'A small girl called Debbie Richards. She was one of the maypole dancers.'

'Ah the maypole.' Nigel was off. 'An ancient sign of fertility. It represents, of course, the phallus, standing straight and erect.'

Potters eyebrows shot up.

'While, of course, the hobby horse is the male predator, trying to pull under his skirts an innocent virgin. Could this have been why the child was murdered? At her age she was bound to have been *virgo intacta*.'

'I don't think so, sir. She was dressed up as a scarecrow at the time.'

'Ah, of course, this definitely has undertones of Wicca. The ancient Greeks used blocks of wood to guard their fields, all carved in the image of Priapus, who was hideously ugly but had a permanent enormous erection. Ever since, the use of men and women made of rags and with, perhaps, a mangel-wurzel for a head, has very dark associations. Very dark indeed.'

'May I sit down?' said Potter.

'Of course, my dear sir. May I offer you some refreshment? A glass of mead perhaps. Very restorative.'

'No, thank you, I am on duty.'

'Of course, of course. You were talking about the murders in the cornfield.'

Potter hadn't the strength to correct him but asked, 'If I may make so bold, sir, where were you last night?'

God, I'm getting to sound like him, Potter thought.

'Last night?' Nigel counted on his fingers. 'Monday. I was out riding my one-eyed steed named Basil.'

'Gracious. May I ask where you do this?'

'Indeed you may. It is over the Downs near Ringmer. I meet up there with fellow knights and we indulge in a small joust and then we repair to an hostelry where we indulge in even further horseplay – if you'll forgive my *jeu de mots* – with the fillies.' He roared with laughter and tightened his tiny eyes.

'And what did you do after that?' continued Potter, fighting with his sanity.

'I repaired to my couch and slept.'

'Alone?'

'Yes, quite alone. There was something boring called the day job looming.'

'I see. And now I would like to talk to you about the first murder. It was done with an arrow and the victim was a boy of ten. He was fixed to the maypole by the ribbons which were wound round him after his death. He was also standing on something which was removed, presumably, before the winding took place. I would very much like to have your comments on the murderer.'

'Well, I don't know who it was but I would reckon that the archer must have gone down on one knee to deliver the shot.'

'I've brought some photographs. Would you like to see them?'

'Like would hardly be the operative word but I shall do so out of a sense of duty.'

Nigel hastily downed another glass of mead while Potter produced the packet of prints. The would-be knight regarded them in a stony silence.

'Um,' he said eventually.

'You have a comment, sir?'

'Well, the arrow entered straight. In other words, it wasn't aimed up or down. This means that the archer was definitely either sitting on the ground or had to be on one knee. He was also reasonably short. As for the victim – may God's mercy receive his soul, amen – he was standing on something – a box, a stool perhaps – which was later removed. Poor little soul. May I suggest that this was a blood sacrifice to ensure the crops go well?'

Inwardly Potter sighed, deeply, but he turned a bright face on Nigel. 'That is something we are looking into Mr Cuthbert-Campbell. We are aware that there are people who still practise devil worship in this remote country area.'

'Yes, but are you aware how seriously they take it? It would not be chivalrous of me to mention any names but look no further than the band of morris men who danced at the fair.'

Potter put on his knowing face and nodded, wondering if by any chance the man could be on to something regarding the blood sacrifice. But there was another line of enquiry that he wished to follow.

'Can you tell me anything about your archers?'

'In what regard?'

'Just their general background.'

Nigel sat up very straight. 'It would be wrong of me to criticize any of my loyal hearts.'

Here we go again, thought Potter, with certain resignation.

'But of them all, Reg Marney is the most troublesome. The other two, Eric and Alan, are married men.' Nigel's little eyes got as close as they ever would to twinkling. 'Though, of course, like all men of the Middle Ages, they have flirtatious encounters – that is all there is to it – with serving wenches.'

'But Reg is more troublesome?'

'Reg lost his wife some years ago and has been indulging in dalliances ever since.' Nigel sighed. 'But, alas, that is the nature of man. To seek comfort at a woman's breast.'

Potter stood up, feeling a little nauseous. 'Well, thank you so much, Mr Cuthbert-Campbell. It has been most enlightening.'

Nigel thrust out a hearty hand. 'A pleasure, young fellow. If ever you should feel like joining The Closed Loop just let me know.'

Potter had a brief mental picture of himself swearing enthusiastic oaths with drunken fellow revellers and shook his head.

'Not for me, sir, though thank you all the same. Too busy with police work I'm afraid.'

Nigel raised his eyebrows in sympathy. 'It was ever thus, my friend. But be of stout heart.'

'I'll try,' answered Potter as he staggered out into the night air.

Belle had been sobbing for the last hour, terrible heart-breaking cries that shook her body involuntarily and caused her skin to grow red and mottled. Melissa felt at the end of her tether, longing for the noise to stop, yet feeling it her duty to sit with her sorrowing granddaughter and pat her hand, murmuring, 'There, there darling,' every so often.

It had all started much earlier in the day when Melissa had been contacted by Susan Richards and told, in an almost unrecognizable voice, that Debbie had been murdered the previous night. Fortunately Hugh had been in and had comforted his wife with all the stoicism of an Afghanistan veteran. But after the initial shock and a couple of stiff drinks, they had turned to one another and realized that Isabelle – out playing with a friend – had to be told.

'I can't face it, Hugh. I truly can't,' Melissa had said, meaning every word.

Hugh had straightened his back. 'Very well. I'll do it.'

He had telephoned his gardening job and cried off and when his granddaughter had come in, little fair plaits swinging out from her head, eyes clear and bright, he had been almost military in his approach.

'Belle, my darling, I have something of a serious nature to tell you.'

'Yes, Daddy?'

'I want you to be a very brave girl, sweet.'

She had looked at him knowingly, momentarily like an adult. 'What is it?'

'I'm sorry, but you won't be able to see Debbie any more.'

'Why not?'

'Because she died last night.' He didn't say anything about how, or where, or any of the grisly details, of which he only knew half himself. 'I'm sorry, Belle. Be a gallant little soldier.'

She had stood silently for a moment before a deluge of tears gushed down her face and her lower lip started quivering.

'Oh, Daddy,' she said, and she had flung herself into his arms.

She had been weeping ever since. In fact Melissa had wondered to herself how one small individual could produce so many tears. She felt every day of her sixty-one years and was tired and unhappy into the bargain.

'Belle, oh my little Belle, can I get you some toast with oozing butter and a nice cup of sweet tea?'

Her granddaughter's body had been racked with an extra loud sob.

'N–n–no, thank you, Mummy.'

'But, sweetheart, you haven't eaten a thing since you came in.'

Belle answered dramatically, 'Debbie hasn't eaten anything, has she, Mummy?'

Melissa stopped her patting and stared at Belle, thinking that the child had been watching the wrong sort of television.

'Now, darling, what made you say that?'

'Well, it's true, isn't it? Dead people don't eat.'

'Well, their bodies don't. But their souls might.'

'I don't believe we go to the arms of Jesus.'

Melissa was silenced, not because of what Belle had just said but because she felt too exhausted to argue. The mystery of whether there was an afterlife was as deep to her as it always had been. Sometimes she believed it, particularly when she thought of genuine clairvoyants and the visions they had. At other times she thought that the human race was just like electric light switches. Turned off. Now she could think of nothing to say. Silently she stood up.

'Where are you going?'

'To get you something to eat. And if you don't want it, I'll have it.'

'Don't leave me, Mummy.'

'Just for a few minutes, darling.'

'I'll be frightened.'

'Why?'

'Because Debbie's ghost might come and haunt me.'

'Nonsense. There are no such things as ghosts.'

'But you saw my father after he had died. I heard you telling Daddy about it.'

'I was imagining it,' said Melissa firmly, and went out of the room, leaving the door ajar. Belle let out such a piercing scream that Hugh came running up the stairs, two at a time.

'What's the matter with her?'

'She thinks Debbie's ghost is coming for her.'

'I'll deal with her. Go downstairs, Melissa, you look done in.'

It was with gratitude that Belle's grandmother made her way to the living room and poured herself a weak gin and tonic before going into the kitchen to stroke Samba, who was purring in his basket.

Dickie Donkin was heading for the coast. He loved the sea, loved its moods and its changing colours. When he had been a boy, he had had a collection of postcards from places with exotic names – he had never known where they had been – but the one thing that attracted him was the differing shades of the mighty ocean. Dazzling peacock from somewhere called Crete, another vivid emerald from Madagascar. All the colours of blue that one could possibly imagine. One he had particularly liked was of a small island surrounded by sapphire waters with a great abbey built on it. It had 'Greetings from Mont St Michel' written on it. Dickie thought now that that had been his favourite.

He knew, though nobody had told him, that the police wanted to question him and that was why he was deliberately going in the opposite direction. They frightened him. They seemed to know things without being told. He knew that they had realized that he had killed his stepfather. But the idea of dumping his weighted clothes in Bewl Water, swimming out to where the reservoir deepened, then swimming naked back to the shore and Farmer Packham's barn to dress in fresh gear, had saved his life. There had been nothing to pin him to the actual murder. And the good old farmer had given him a firm alibi. Said he had looked in during the night and seen Dickie sleeping like a babe.

The tramp smiled at that memory and walked resolutely on, his goal to get to Fairlight Glen, where he could rest a little and contemplate the ocean. Aching though his feet were, he plodded onwards until eventually he left the houses behind and there, overlooking the mighty monster – as he affectionately nicknamed the sea – someone had thoughtfully put a wooden seat, big enough for three. 'In Memory of Alf Adkins who sat in this spot daily' had been written on a small plaque attached to the back. Thinking of Alf, Dickie had lain down on the bench and fallen asleep.

He awoke slowly, muzzy as usual, but after blinking his eyes several times he saw that someone was leaning over him and smiling. Dickie smiled back, showing his rotting brown teeth.

'Hello, sonny. Having a little kip, were we?'

Dickie swung his legs down and looked earnestly at the person speaking to him. It was a schoolboy dressed in a uniform of some kind. And then slowly the fog from his brain lifted. It was a policeman. Instinctively Dickie started to run but there was a restraining hand on his shoulder.

'You're Richard Donkin, aren't you?' said the boy.

Dickie nodded. The game was up. There was no point in struggling.

'Don't be frightened,' the boy said very gently. 'We just want to ask you a few questions, that's all.'

A tear ran down Dickie's dirty cheek as the handcuffs were put on him and he was led to a nearby police car where a small girl dressed as a policewoman got out and stared at him.

'Did he cause any trouble?' she asked.

The boy laughed. 'No. He's as gentle as a lamb, aren't you, Dickie?'

Dickie nodded. 'Yes,' came out of the cavern of his throat, and he managed to smile at the boy once more.

Jack Boggis was holding forth loudly. 'I tell you that this damned village is haunted. Talk about *Midsomer Murders*. I should think the author – whoever he or she was – must have based it on Lakehurst. Another child last night! I'm seriously thinking of putting my house on the market.'

'Goodie!' shouted an unseen listener from the bar.

Jack shot them a look of pure malice and took a sup of ale. 'As I was saying, Doctor, it really isn't a village fit to live in.'

'Well,' began Kasper in his beautiful accented voice, 'these particular murders are taking place outside. I mean, those fields belong to Sir Rufus Beaudegrave. They are not, strictly speaking, part of Lakehurst.'

'They're near enough. In my opinion there's a madman on the loose. He's clearly a child-hater and a danger to the whole community.'

'You're hardly a child, Mr Boggis. If your theory is right, you have nothing to fear.'

'And that's telling you,' shouted the unseen listener.

The vicar walked in quietly and stood listening to the exchange of words. In other circumstances he would have been smiling, because Jack Boggis was such an old woman in his opinion, but tonight he felt stretched to his limit. The murder of two innocent children on two consecutive nights had shocked him profoundly. He had been to church and prayed that the malefactor would be caught, that the babes would be received in the hereafter, that harmony could soon be restored to the village. And he had felt slightly guilty because however hard he concentrated on the presence of evil, glorious golden Patsy had crept into his thoughts and he had wished that she lived close to him so that he could have confided his feelings to her.

Kasper spoke. 'If you are feeling nervous, Mr Boggis, perhaps you could come into my surgery and I will give you a prescription.'

Jack had snorted like an angry old mule. 'Tranquilizers. I don't want any of them things, thank you all the same. Ruin you once you start on those. I knew a woman once who was still on some anti-depressant thirty years after her husband died. And still going on about feeling on the verge of suicide.'

'You will always get those types, of course,' Kasper said sadly.

'May I join you?' asked Nick.

'All right,' answered Boggis, none too affably.

'I heard what you said just now and have met quite a few of them in my time,' the vicar added. 'I think they are attention-seekers deep down.'

'Not so deep,' Jack answered gloomily. 'They dine out on being ill. As my old father used to say, "They enjoy bad health".'

'Well, at least they enjoyed something,' shouted the wag from the bar, and there was general laughter.

Nick was vividly reminded of just how tough a creature mankind was. Here was this small village in Sussex, currently threatened by some evil being who could murder children and dress them up like some obscene sacrifice, yet in the face of all that the residents could still find something to laugh about. That surely must be the greatest blessing of all; that in the face of danger and menace they could still retain their sense of humour. He raised his glass to the unseen joker and said 'Cheers'.

SIXTEEN

Tennant gently removed his arms from the lovely warm body of Olivia and fifteen minutes later crept out of her house and was on the road to Lewes. He called in at his own flat, had a shower and put on some different clothes. Then he drove into the police headquarters and spent two hours on the computer. He looked through every case of child murder that had happened anywhere in the United Kingdom in the last ten years, but could find nothing quite as freakish as this. He looked through all the reports of the house-to-house calls made in the village of Lakehurst and its surrounding dwellings. He then brought up on the screen the case of the murder of George Munn and the interviews with his stepson, who was the number one suspect. Admittedly Dickie's fingerprints were round the cottage but then he had lived there as a boy until the horrible attack which had hospitalized both him and his mother.

That had been when Dickie was fifteen but George had not cleaned the house much and it was not enough to get a conviction. As for Dickie's alibi, it was cast iron. Jacob Packham had sworn that he had looked in his barn twice and had seen Dickie sleeping in the hay. Reluctantly, the case had been dropped.

Now he had been arrested again. He had been spotted by a patrol car in the unlikely place of Fairlight Glen and had been brought into the nearest police station. He had spent the night in the cells – poor bugger, thought Tennant – and was being transferred to Lewes in the morning. Tennant considered Dickie seriously for a moment or two and his instinct told him that the man was harmless. Autistic but harmless. He decided to leave the first interview to Potter and he would tell him to go easy on the poor old sod. Tennant made a note to himself to call in the psychiatrist who worked with cases of autism. Having done this, he got into his car and headed back to Lakehurst.

On arrival he was pleased to see Potter there ahead of him.

'Mark, what brings you out so early?'

'I spent most of the night patrolling the fields. And before you say anything, sir, I know you didn't ask me but I just wanted to check that the lunatic wasn't going to strike for the third time.'

'That was good of you. By the way, go and get one of the WPCs to have another word with Miss Dunkley. She must have gut instincts about this case.'

'Talking of instincts I went to interview the chief of the archers last night. It took me an hour to recover! But he does have one interesting theory.'

'Which is?'

'That the children were blood sacrifices to ensure that the crops would be good. It's an old ritual apparently.'

'I wonder,' answered Tennant.

'What?'

'Sussex is full of ancient beliefs and according to Chris O'Hare they are still very much alive and kicking.'

'Are you going to see him or shall I?'

'Me. I want you to go to Lewes. They've arrested Richard Donkin apparently. I want you to interview him very gently. You probably won't get anything out of him, he barely speaks.'

'No, but he can sing. So the vicar told me.'

Tennant laughed aloud. 'Perhaps you should base your enquiries on an opera.'

'Which one?'

'*The Knot Garden*, perhaps.'

'Are you serious?'

'Very. Tippett was the composer.'

'I should have thought something more light-hearted.'

'Try *Land of Smiles*,' said Tennant, and grinned to himself at Mark Potter's expression of total incredulity. 'Or perhaps *La Wally* might be more up your street.'

Melissa thought that she had never known such a terrible night. It was so awful that early the next morning Hugh had called Dr Rudniski to their house to give Isabelle a sedative. The child was hysterical, refusing to sleep or to be left alone, saying that the ghost of Debbie was coming to torment her if they left her by herself. He had given Isabelle an injection which she had attempted to avoid, threshing round the bed until Hugh had held her down.

Twenty minutes later and the fretful child was out cold. The three adults had gone downstairs and stared at one another.

'Of course, it is understandable,' said the doctor. 'She has lost her best friend in a horrible way. It is no wonder that she is upset.'

Melissa thought that had she been twenty years younger – and single – she would have found him dashingly attractive and wondered why he wasn't in a relationship. But then she thought that generally speaking the young women of Lakehurst were nothing special, which the Polish doctor definitely was. She stood up.

'It was very good of you to come and visit us at this early hour. Let me get you some coffee.'

The clock was striking seven as she came in bearing a tray with coffee and a selection of biscuits. Hugh was speaking.

'It has been a bit of a problem coping with a youngster. I particularly worry about the effect on Melissa.'

'Don't fret about me, darling, she has been a real joy. That is, most of the time.'

Kasper, looking at her, thought she looked drawn and tired, but small wonder when she had been up all night with a screaming child.

'I do not wish to speak out of turn, Mrs Wyatt, but I think perhaps you should get away for a few days. It would do you good. Lakehurst is not a happy place to be at the moment.'

'But I can't leave Hugh on his own. Not with Belle in her present state. It wouldn't be fair.'

'Nonsense, my darling, I've looked after a battalion before now. One nervy little girl is nothing by comparison. I think you should go to your sister's.'

'I'm sorry, Hugh. I'm not going and that is that.' She turned to the doctor. 'How do you like your coffee?'

'Black without sugar, please.'

'Of course. Very wise. No additives.'

They sat in silence, Hugh munching on a biscuit, the doctor thinking about the whole sad set-up and just wishing he could do something more than give Belle injections to take away her horrific fantasies.

* * *

Dickie Donkin was terribly sad. In fact, he felt at his lowest ebb. He had spent the night in a horrible cell, which stank with the odour of its former resident. The bed had been hard, the lavatory grim, the whole place giving him a sense of being like a caged bird when he was a man born to roam the country. Yet it had happened to him before and he had been set free that time.

I've got to play my cards right, he thought. He had no idea what the words actually meant, though it was good to think them, that was for sure. He had been given breakfast that morning and had made an effort at washing himself, running a damp flannel over his neck and dabbing it under his arms. Then he had sat on the bunk and waited to be called.

He had quite enjoyed the ride from the police station to Lewes but by the time he was seated in a room on his own, he was nervous again. Dickie didn't like being enclosed and this was just how it felt to him. As if he was going to be locked in this little room for eternity. And then to his amazement he heard somebody singing, just a snatch of song but it was immensely cheering. He strained his ears and at that moment the door opened and the singing stopped, though the three people who had come into the room were all humming. Dickie looked up at them, half raising his eyelids.

There was only one dressed like a policeman and Dickie thought he was about sixteen at the most. The other two were in civvies and the older man sat down next to him and said pleasantly, 'Hello, Dickie. I am a solicitor and I am here to represent you.'

Dickie made a protesting movement and Potter went on to say, 'It's all right, Dickie. Mr Dovell is a friend of Mr Tennant's. You won't have to pay him anything. Neither of them, I mean. They are doing this because they like you.'

Dickie couldn't understand it. He knew that lawyers were things that you had to buy. But he stopped thinking about that as Potter switched a little machine on and said a few preliminary words into it.

Then, 'Are you Richard Donkin?' he asked.

Dickie stared at him, and finally nodded his head.

'Can you tell me where you were on Saturday, May the first this year, between the hours of three p.m. and the following morning?'

Dickie looked blank and Mr Dovell, who had met Tennant and liked him while they had both been attending the Police Law course at Hendon, said, 'Come on, son, don't be shy. Just tell us, did you go to the fair?'

Dickie shook his head and growled, 'Trees.'

'What about them? Were you watching from them?' said Potter.

'I dances,' said Dickie with great effort.

'Switch the recorder off a minute,' said Alasdair Dovell. 'Listen, Dickie, if we ask you questions about where you were, could you just answer by nodding or shaking your head?'

A pair of blue eyes, vacant and somehow profoundly sad, stared into Alasdair's with a beseeching glance. Dickie nodded.

Alasdair spoke to Potter. 'Would that be all right for you, Sergeant? I mean, I think it's as far as we're going to get, otherwise.'

'Yes, I felt sure we were going to have to compromise when this interview began.' Potter turned to Dickie again. 'When the fair ended did you stay in the woods?'

Definite nodding of head. Alasdair said, 'My client indicated yes.'

'And did you go to the Great House afterwards and sit outside?'

Terrific nodding of head.

'And what did you do then, Dickie? Did you go back to the woods?'

Dickie hesitated, then seizing a piece of paper lying on the desk, looked round pleadingly.

'I think he wants a pen,' said Alasdair.

'I'm just glad my boss isn't here,' said Potter, reluctantly handing Dickie a biro.

Then all three present onlookers grew silent as they watched in amazement as he drew a portrait of a road, a morris dancer dressed in tatters, a black hat on his head ringed with a row of pheasant feathers, and a girl dressed in white, standing, looking across the fields into the dim distance.

'Skye,' said Potter.

'What?' said Alasdair.

'Chris O'Hare kept rattling on about trying to pick up some posh totty named Skye. He apparently did not succeed but after tempting her to walk a little way with him she turned and left.

So far, nobody seems to know who she is and house-to-house hasn't revealed her whereabouts either.'

Alasdair turned to Dickie. 'Are you showing us that Skye went off in the direction of the murder? Is that what it is, Dickie?'

There was a silence that seemed to last for ever while Daft Dickie pondered what had just been asked him. Then he turned to Potter, every vein on his face standing out, and from a throat that sounded as dry as the Sahara Desert rasped out, 'Yes.'

'You didn't push him too hard?' said Tennant, when Potter rejoined him at the Lakehurst incident room.

'On the contrary, sir. We all entered humming like Madame Butterfly on a bad night, and he ended up by drawing for us a mysterious picture set at the crossroads. Here it is.'

'My God,' Tennant exclaimed.

'What?'

'He's actually got talent. It looks like the later work of van Gogh. He could make a fortune selling these.'

'But does it tell us anything?'

'Not really. The carer from the children's home says he – Ned – hurried straight home.' Tennant changed tone. 'We've got to find Skye, Potter. I think she might hold the key to the whole thing.'

'But how do we find her? She might have been a day tripper come from London.'

'And she might just as easily not. I've got a hunch, Potter. Do you feel like a pint at lunchtime?'

'I could do with one certainly.'

They made their way to the Great House rather earlier than usual and Dominic looked round immediately for Jack Boggis, rather fearing that they might have beaten the old toper to it. But they were in luck. Jack was in his usual chair, back turned to the general public, *Daily Telegraph* spread before him, quaffing his ale like an old soldier. Tennant braved the usual rebuff and sat down opposite him, flicking at Jack's paper and saying, 'Peep-bo, Mr Boggis. I'd like to speak to you.'

The newspaper quivered with annoyance and eventually Boggis laid it down, fury flying from his fingertips.

'Well?' he said.

'Yes, very, thank you. How about yourself?'

'I was reading a very interesting article until I was interrupted.'

'May I offer you a pint to make redress? I see by your smile that I can.'

Boggis's lips were drawn back in a snarl.

'Good,' Tennant hurried on. He looked contrite. 'The reason I sought you out is a serious one, and it's on account of your tremendous powers of observation.'

Boggis glared.

'I need your help, sir, and I need it desperately.'

Boggis chuffed like a pug but Tennant was unable to translate the sound and continued.

'I am relying on your powers of noticing things, sir, with reference to the night of the Medieval Fair. I know you were in this pub and I expect you saw many familiar faces in here. But it is one in particular that I am interested in and that is the blackened-up face of a morris dancer, Chris O'Hare. Did you notice him, by any chance?'

'And if I did?'

'Potter, go and get Mr Boggis a pint of ale, there's a good chap. Now, as I was saying, did you?'

'Yes, he walked past me in order to find a seat.'

'And did he have a woman with him?'

'Yes. A pretty young thing in a long white dress.'

'Did you recognize her?'

'No. She had one of those highfalutin' Venetian carnival masks on. All I could see was her chin and her forehead.'

'What about her hair?'

'That was gathered up in one of those golden snood affairs. But it was dark, I could see that much.'

Tennant received one of those odd premonitions which he had occasionally had in the past. He suddenly felt certain that he knew who Skye was. But he showed none of this to Jack Boggis, who was looking as if he were longing to get back to his paper. Tennant got to his feet.

'Well, thank you very much, Mr Boggis. You have been as helpful and kind as always,' he said, keeping his face absolutely straight.

Boggis shot him a quizzical look but Tennant was leaving the pub, with young Potter solemnly bowing his head in the doorway.

'Bloody fools,' Boggis muttered, as he re-opened his favourite newspaper and started to read.

Outside in the car Tennant said, 'I want you to go and find O'Hare at the garage and give him a hard time. See if you can learn any more about this blood sacrifice thing. Ask him if he is the leader of a coven?'

'And where will you be, sir?'

'I've got a couple of calls to make. We'll meet up again at Lewes about six.'

'Very good. I'll find out more about our dwarfish archer too while I'm at it. See if he noticed anything while he was having a quickie in the woods.'

Tennant guffawed. 'I shouldn't imagine you'll get much response there. I mean, one doesn't do a lot of looking around. You've other things on your mind.'

'I'll take your word for it, sir,' Mark said cheekily, and drove off.

Susan Richards was in a state of terrible tension. To add to her crippling sorrow that Debbie should have been cut down by some depraved assailant, her younger child, Johnnie, had now gone into a state resembling a catatonic trance. He lay in bed, not moving nor eating, not even going to the lavatory. His eyes were fixed on the ceiling and he made no response to Susan's increasing efforts to stimulate him. She rang Dr Rudniski in barely controlled hysteria and he assured her that he would come immediately. In fact, he appeared thirty minutes later, by which time Susan had consumed half a bottle of wine and was feeling somewhat better.

He gave Johnnie an intra-muscular injection to let the boy get some sleep and afterwards came down to talk seriously to Susan.

'It is obvious that Johnnie has taken the death of his sister really hard. But why should he have done that, do you think?'

Susan stared at him and said, 'Why do you think? He's in mourning for her, of course.'

'Please excuse me, Mrs Richards, my English is not perfect.

I have seen many children in mourning but none have ever taken the form of Johnnie's. I feel that there is some additional thing. For example, he did not see her murdered, did he?'

'No, no he didn't.' And then Susan stopped and sat thinking. 'At least, I don't believe so. But then I was asleep most of that night. Oh God, I should have checked his room. Perhaps you're right. Oh, Doctor, it's all my fault.'

Kasper's big Polish heart bled for her. He hated seeing women in distress, particularly this poor wretch whose world seemed to have come to a terrible end. He sat quietly for a minute or two, then said, 'Can your ex-husband not help you? He should be here at a time like this. You have told him?'

'I phoned him today, after I got back from Lewes. I didn't speak to him. She answered. Scarlett, his mistress. So I sent him a text but he hasn't replied.'

'I can telephone if you wish. I can tell him that you no longer should be left alone.'

'But then he will bring that horrible Scarlett. If he comes at all.'

'I can tell him not to bring her,' answered Kasper, assuming more authority than he actually had.

Susan smiled weakly. 'I don't think he'll listen.'

'May I ask the whereabouts of WPC Jones?'

'I think she has gone to the Incident Room. She won't be long.'

'Ask her to ring me when she returns. I would like to speak to her. Meanwhile, leave Johnnie to sleep. I shall be here first thing tomorrow morning to check on him. And, Mrs Richards . . .'

'Yes?'

'Don't drink too much. You will feel worse if you have a hangover in the morning.'

Major Wyatt had decided to keep his appointment with old Mrs Chambers, whose garden he attended once a week. She was a sprightly pensioner with a razor-sharp memory and a rather amusing line in conversation. Frankly, once he had assured himself that Melissa could cope with the situation at home, he had set out on his bicycle, his gardening tools in a bag slung across the handlebars.

Mrs Chambers dwelled in a small cottage which had once belonged to an agricultural worker on the Beaudegrave estate. But these had long since been sold off and fortunately the house was semi-detached so the old lady had a couple of arty neighbours who came down at weekends. They were able to check on her well-being but Hugh still worried that an elderly woman should live in such an isolated position. However, she was trimming the hedge as he arrived and gave no sign at all of being of advancing years.

'Ah, Major, good morning to you. You're just in time for a cup of tea. Or would you prefer coffee?'

'Whatever you're having, Mrs Chambers. Thank you so much.'

She led him into her chintzy kitchen and ushered him on to the window seat. 'Well, what do you think?' she said.

'About the murders, you mean?'

'Yes, of course. Were you at the Medieval Fair?'

'Indeed I was. My granddaughter, Isabelle, was dancing round the maypole. I wouldn't have missed it for the world. But it was a terrible business, what happened afterwards. Absolutely terrible.'

'Yes. Of course, I could see it from my bedroom window. Only in the distance, but still visible.'

'I didn't realize that,' said the major, sipping his tea and wondering what was coming next.

'Funnily enough, that was one of the nights when I had a bad turn of insomnia. I've been suffering from it for years, you know. The doctor gives me pills but sometimes I just can't sleep for toffee. So I read instead.'

'I see,' answered Hugh, hoping that she was going to tell him something further. He was not to be disappointed.

'That night – I refer to the night after the fair when the murder happened – I looked out of my window at the scene of so much earlier merriment . . .'

'Yes?'

'And I saw something.'

'What?'

'Two figures dancing round the maypole, while a third figure looked on.'

'My God, could you see who they were?'

'No, that I couldn't tell. But I definitely saw them. It was not a dream.'

'Have you told the police about this, Mrs Chambers?'

'Do you think I should?'

'Definitely. Could you make out who they were? I mean, what sex or what age? Personal facts?'

'No, I couldn't see the details. Just people.'

'Did you happen to notice the time?'

'Yes, it was three in the morning. The grandfather struck in the hall below.'

Hugh made up his mind. 'Come along, Mrs Chambers. We're going to get in your car and I am going to drive you to the police incident room. I think this is vital information and you must pass it on immediately.'

'Do you really think so?'

'Yes,' answered the major. 'I really, really do.'

SEVENTEEN

Tennant had been thinking of calling on Melissa Wyatt and her hysterical granddaughter but had changed his mind halfway. He sincerely hoped that the child had settled down by now but, quite frankly, did not feel in the mood for the sound of distant weeping. Feeling a bit of a sissy he nonetheless drove resolutely on till he finally perceived the outlines of the castle rising in the near distance. It impressed him every time he saw it. There was something so solemn and so grand about it that it never failed to make him catch his breath. He slowed down so that he could take in something of its wondrous beauty.

At this time of year the wildfowl on its impressive moat were busy building nests along the bank. Elegant black swans sailed along, the water on their feathers glistening like crystal in the sunshine. Tennant stopped the car and got out to look at them, feeling childish for doing so but wanting a moment alone to absorb the gorgeous palette of colour that nature was providing on this most beautiful day. Ducks chugged along, looking beside the larger waterfowl like the tugs drawing *Titanic* on its first – and last – voyage out to sea. Moorhens dipped their heads and raised them in their inimitable way. White swans glided over the moat like the regal and beautiful birds they were. It was heavenly. Nature at its most productive and graceful. Tennant loitered, partly because the loveliness was overwhelming, partly because he had a tricky job to do inside and he wanted no ruffled feathers of the human sort.

Knocking on the door of the private part of the castle, the Victorian buildings where the family lived, it was answered by Sir Rufus's fiancée, the gorgeous Ekaterina, looking even more stunning than when they had first met eighteen months earlier. He realized that it was happiness that had added the finishing touches to the portrait, the splendour that can only come from within. There and then, with no preconceived plan at all, he decided to ask her advice.

Unaware, Ekaterina said, 'Dear Inspector Tennant, how nice to see you. I'm just having some tea, would you like some? I do hope that this is purely a social call.'

'Partly, I must confess. There's something I want to talk to you about.'

'Oh, dear.'

She picked up the house phone and ordered tea, meanwhile beckoning him into a comfortable chair. They had been placed in their summer position by the long windows overlooking the moat and once again Tennant cast his eyes on the beautiful panorama but from a different perspective.

'Well, now,' she said. 'What does my favourite policeman want with me?'

'Before we get down to business, I must tell you that you look absolutely radiant, Ekaterina.'

'For the first time in my life I am really happy. Did you know that Rufus and I are getting married in September? You promise to come?'

'Where and when, exactly?'

'The second Saturday. There is to be a small ceremony in Chelsea Register Office and then Nick, dear Nick, is going to bless our marriage in the chapel here in the castle. And afterward there will be a reception in the Tudor dining hall.'

'Sounds wonderful. I shall take a day's leave.'

'And your darling Mark Potter, he must come too. My four girls will act as bridesmaids and it will be such a joyful occasion.'

'It is about your girls that I wanted to talk to you. The eldest one, in fact.'

Ekaterina's face changed, looking so doleful that Dominic felt obliged to say, 'It's nothing serious, I assure you.'

It was at this moment that the tea tray arrived and it wasn't until they were settled with cups that Dominic said, 'You remember the day of the Medieval Fair?'

'Of course I do. The two big girls ran a stall and we all dressed up. It was a lovely fair, but to think it should end in terrible tragedy . . .'

Tennant leant forward. 'Please don't misunderstand me, Ekaterina. But I wanted to ask about Araminta. When she had finished with the stall and the fair ended, do you know if she went to the Great House pub?'

'Yes, I think she told Rufus she was going. She is eighteen now, Dominic. She can do what she likes.'

'Do you know if she covered her face with a Venetian mask?'

'Well, she's got one. I don't know whether she had it with her. Possibly. Why?'

'Because a young woman answering her description was seen talking to a Mr O'Hare, who leads the morris dancers, Mr Grimm's Men.'

Ekaterina looked at him with misty blue eyes. 'So did she do something wrong?'

'Not wrong exactly. It is Mr O'Hare that we are interested in. I would just like to hear her side of the conversation.'

He left out the fact that she had been seen walking away from the dancer when the young man who worked at the children's home had been out for a late-night cigarette.

Ekaterina finished her cup and looked pleased. 'I am glad that is all. I would not like to think she is in trouble of any kind. I regard her as my stepdaughter now – and soon she will legally be so.' Tennant smiled but did not answer and Ekaterina said, 'I will ring her room on the house phone. Excuse me.'

She phoned through and the call was obviously picked up.

'My darling girl, that nice Inspector Tennant is here and he wants to speak to you. No, I don't know what it is about. Darling, I really think you should. Shall I tell him you will meet him in the Georgian parlour? Oh, thank you. Yes, I'll say.'

She gave the inspector a slightly conspiratorial smile. 'She says she is in a hurry because she is going out, but she can spare five minutes. I'll take you to the Georgian part of the castle now.'

As he walked behind her, Dominic looked grim. He wished he had a five-pound note for every stroppy teenager he had been forced to interview in his long progress to inspector. Young tarts, boys high on drugs, negligent blacks, rude whites, and aggressive creatures of every size and description. At least Araminta was going to be polite.

She was already seated but rose and shook his hand.

'Hello, Inspector. Nice to see you again.'

'And you too, Miss Beaudegrave.'

She did not say 'Call me Araminta' as he had hoped.

'How can I help you?' she said now, icily polite.

Dominic decided to be cold and direct.

'I have had a report, Miss Beaudegrave, that you were seen talking to Christopher O'Hare at some extremely late hour on the night of the first murder.'

She went terribly pale, looking like Snow White with her ashen skin stark against her jet-black hair. 'I see,' she said in a whisper.

'Well?' asked Tennant, sparing her nothing.

'It is true that I met him at the fair and he invited me to go and have a drink with him afterwards in the Great House.'

'Was this your first meeting or had you known him before?'

'No, I met him at the fair. I congratulated him on his dancing. I liked it a lot.'

'I see. And tell me, where did you go after the drink was finished?'

She went from pale to waxen. 'Nowhere. Just out for a walk.'

He leant towards her. 'Look, Araminta, I'm not trying to get at you. What you do is your own affair and entirely up to you. What I am interested in is did you see anybody when you were out on this walk? Did you pass anyone? Those are the sort of facts I need to have.'

She looked at him with eyes that were very wide and honest. 'Well, I did pass that old tramp that's always hanging round the place. And the young chap from the children's home.'

'Anybody else?'

'Well, I didn't actually pass them but I could hear little whispers coming from the hedge.'

'What do you mean?'

'I think there were some children about – or else it was adults doing children's voices. Anyway, I could hear them whispering to one another. Chris started to look for them but then Ned came up and I thought he'd come to fetch them. And anyway Chris had started getting a bit . . . well, you know. And I wasn't interested so I went back to the pub and fetched my car from the car park.'

'And drove home?'

'Yes. But I had to brake really hard on the way back because a ghostly figure ran across the road in front of me.'

'Who was it? Do you know?'

'No, honestly. I think it was a ghost because I didn't hit anyone and when I peered round it had gone.'

'How frightening.'

'I tell you, my flesh was creeping when I had to let myself into the castle. Fortunately Daddy had left the lights on, otherwise I think I would have had hysterics.'

'Is the castle haunted?' asked Tennant, genuinely interested.

'Massively,' and Araminta smiled for the first time.

'Tell me.'

'Well, the medieval bit is packed with them but I've never seen them because we don't go wandering round that part on our own after dark. It's out of bounds – and I still obey the rules.'

She gave Tennant a smile full of secret meaning and he thought he understood and grinned back.

'But one I have seen – well, two actually – are a sad little girl who used to come and watch us when we were playing. We used to be frightened of her but in the end if she came we just said, "Oh, there's Alice", and continued with whatever it was that we were doing.'

'And the second?'

'Well, you're not going to believe this but all five of us have seen her. She sits in the Georgian dining room at the head of the table. She has a powdered wig on and looks just as if she's stepped off the set of some old black and white film. Whenever she's appeared – and that's about six times to my knowledge – she always bows her head graciously and smiles, showing tiny little seed-pearl teeth. And then she sort of fades out. But she always comes when something lucky is going to happen. We call her Lady Luck, which is a bit corny, but there it is.'

'Your father has seen her?'

'Yes, just before he met Ekaterina. So he believes in her too.'

'To get back to the ghost that ran in front of your car. Tell me exactly what you saw.'

'A frightened-looking little boy ran across the road directly in front of me. He glanced at me for a second and then he disappeared.'

'What was he wearing?'

'Short trousers and a white shirt.'

Tennant nodded, sure that she had seen Billy. 'The fact that he vanished, could that have been because he was pulled into the hedge?'

Araminta frowned. 'It could have been. I was concentrating so hard on doing an emergency stop that all my attention went on that.'

The inspector got up, ready to go, then he turned to the young woman. 'If you don't mind me saying, you're a great girl, Miss Beaudegrave. Don't waste yourself on the Chris O'Hares of this world. Find yourself a really nice young man.'

'But I don't want to marry a chinless wonder, as my grandmother used to call them.'

'There are plenty out there who'll suit you. It's just a question of taking your time.'

She laughed and said, 'Will you marry me, Inspector?'

'If I was twenty years younger I would do so like a shot.'

As he was driving over the footbridge his mobile rang and Potter's voice spoke over the ether.

'Boss, there's been a development. Mrs Chambers, who lives at the farm close to the murder spot, saw people dancing round the maypole. In the middle of the night.'

'Can she identify them?'

'No, but she said there were two of them.'

'I'll go and see her directly. Give me her address.'

Potter dictated it, then added, 'She's pretty old but she's sharp as a blade.'

'Sounds like my own mama. I look forward to meeting her.'

The sun had lost a little of its brilliance as Dominic Tennant drove down the lane to the pair of farmworkers' cottages, whitewashed, both with wooden porches smothered with rosebuds getting ready to burst into bloom.

He thought it rather an isolated spot and felt worried about Mrs Chambers, whose only neighbours were weekenders. He decided to put an unobtrusive police guard on the cottage until the investigation was over.

'Oh, good evening, Inspector. Sergeant Potter just rang and told me you were on your way.'

Tennant shook her extended hand. 'Good evening, Mrs Chambers. What a lovely cottage – and what a lovely spot.'

'Yes, it is. Sussex is such a beautiful county. I adore living here.'

Tennant smiled wryly, thinking of the ugliness that lay beneath the surface everywhere. Why, oh why, did mankind have to ruin the natural beauty all around? He thought of the indescribable perfection of a blossom tree and then thought of a lout vomiting in the street on a Saturday night. I'm in the wrong job, he considered for the millionth time.

Mrs Chambers insisted that he have a small glass of sherry before conducting him up to her bedroom and showing him the view from her window. Tennant could still see the maypole and various figures in white wandering about.

'I notice the forensics crowd are still at work.'

'Oh yes, they're so wonderful. What did we do before them?'

'Well, they've been around in various early forms for quite a while now. But today's teams are exemplary. In my opinion, anyway.'

'Oh, I couldn't agree more. I move my chair by the window and sit and watch them for hours on end.'

'And casting your mind back to the night of the first murder, you really couldn't see their faces at all?'

'No. I couldn't. But I got the impression that they were all quite short. But that was probably a distortion due to the distance.'

'Yes, I see what you mean.'

Very, very faintly a bell tinkled in the back of Tennant's mind. But it was a true will-o'-the-wisp and was gone as he tried to form the idea. Nevertheless he fell silent.

'Another glass of sherry, Inspector?'

'Thank you, but no. I must go back to the incident room and talk to Potter before I go home.'

'Do you live far away?'

'I have an apartment in Lewes but I am staying with a friend during the course of the investigation.'

'Oh, good. That must save you a lot of driving.'

Tennant grinned at her. 'It is very pleasant, you can rest assured.'

Potter was grim but determined. He had made four attempts to call on Chris O'Hare and every time nobody had answered the door. And, moreover, there had been no sound from inside the house and he felt certain that it was temporarily empty. There was nothing for it but to drive back to Lewes.

He had seen his boss in the incident room and they had compared notes and looked briefly at the computers. There was no new information and both men had the nasty feeling that the case was beginning to stall.

'I've put a guard on Mrs Chambers,' Tennant had said.

'Why, other than for the fact she's a bit isolated?'

'That, but I think that she knows more than she is saying.'

'You mean she's withholding evidence?' Potter had asked incredulously.

'Not deliberately. But I feel certain that she has seen something but is discounting it.'

Potter had shaken his head, not certain what to make of that remark and now, driving through the depths of Speckled Wood, he was still puzzling about it. He thought of the inspector, safely tucked in for the night at Olivia's cottage, and envied him. His – Potter's – trouble was that the run-of-the-mill girls he met just didn't do a thing for him. He wanted someone different, a girl with brains, not one of the present lookalike brigade, flashing their leggings and their shellacked nails about the place. But he supposed that was all he was destined to meet and felt infinitely sad.

He had found a quick route home by cutting through the deep woods that ran down to the sea and then making a sharp left turn. And he was just about to do this when he became aware of a glow to his right. Thinking it might be a fire, Potter stopped the car and got out, suddenly becoming terribly aware of the sounds of the night, the rustlings and slitherings, the sharp, quick, little snapping of twigs. He crept forward towards the glow, conscious of the noise of his own breathing.

A ring of lanterns had been placed in a circle within which stood a group of people, stark naked except for the masks over their faces. Potter gawped, amazed. There was a great deal of pubic hair which glistened in the faint light as the circle started to dance slowly round. They linked hands and chanted, a noise that sounded like 'Rah, rah, rah', which was so incongruous that Potter felt a grin start to creep over his face. There were some women with rolls of fat hanging on their backs and others that looked as if they had come from a concentration camp. But of one person's identity he could be absolutely sure. The peroxide locks of Chris O'Hare were glistening in the uncertain light.

It all looked quite harmless until one young woman went into the midst of the circle and was crowned with a circlet of black laurel leaves. Then a male came forward, extremely erect, and they proceeded to have sex, standing up, and very much in public.

Potter was not quite sure what to do. He didn't feel like taking on a group of rampant – in every sense – males, so decided to leave while the going was good, which it clearly was for the couple in the middle, who were having a whale of a time. He began to back out quietly and then he saw a blond head turn in his direction. He had been seen by Chris O'Hare. Potter took to his heels and ran, not feeling safe until he was in his car and driving hell-for-leather in the direction of his home town. Had he been recognized? He was not certain. But he now had the proof he had been looking for. Chris had a coven that got up to fairly harmless high jinks in the woods.

EIGHTEEN

Life, for the Reverend Nicholas Lawrence, seemed to have deteriorated into a humdrum round of parish duties. But thank God for them, for they kept his mind from wandering to thoughts of the girl who had entered it and refused to go away. Nick was prepared to admit that he was thoroughly preoccupied with the unusual and creative Patsy Quinn. But tonight the organizing committee of the Medieval Fair were to meet at the vicarage for their debriefing, as Nick had once laughingly called it. Now his laughter had been silenced. He knew that this was going to be the most miserable meeting of all.

One by one they trooped in, all wearing a pall of gloom and speaking in quiet voices. The bell rang again and Nick discovered Hugh Wyatt standing on the doorstep, but was not so pleased to see Melissa and Isabelle standing behind him.

'So sorry I had to bring the family,' he said in an undertone. 'Quite frankly, Melissa gets a bit nervous being left on her own. We're rather isolated.'

'Of course, of course. Come in. Would you like to watch television in my living room, Belle? There's only the old cat in there at the moment.'

'Thank you, Father Lawrence,' she said, and allowed him to get her settled on the sofa.

Meanwhile the doorbell kept ringing and Hugh stepped into the breach while Nick bustled about handing round refreshments. Melissa, looking quite dreadful, pale, drawn and with suitcases under her eyes – as Nick's mother used to say – sat apart listlessly, not even offering to help hand round the small glasses of sherry that Nick had felt appropriate to cheer the mood. The doorbell rang once more and Hugh went to answer it.

'Oh, I hope it's not inconvenient,' said a voice with a lift in it. 'I've come to see Father Nick.'

Nick knew, his mother being very fond of musicals, that there was a ridiculous song from *Kismet* which said something about nightingales singing at noon on the mulberry bough, and moment-arily believed it was true. He felt that he glided towards the front door and stood bowing and blushing and generally behaving like a total idiot as he kissed the hand of the wonderful, the beautiful, the totally unexpected Miss Patsy Quinn.

He ushered her into the meeting and there was a general buzz of curiosity.

'Miss Quinn, who I'm sure you'll remember opening the fair for us.'

There was a universal swell of conversation and Nick, just for a moment, felt frozen in time and knew, quite certainly, that he was going to marry her and live contentedly ever after. That is, of course, providing that she wanted to marry him.

Popping his head round the living room door, he saw Belle watching something quite unsuitable on television with Radetsky purring on her lap.

'I'll bring you some biscuits and lemonade,' he said and she turned and smiled at him in quite an adult way.

The evening went well, considering the awful aftermath of the fair, to say nothing of the second murder in the field beyond. It was as if the spirits of everyone had been raised by the arrival of Miss Quinn and Nick was fairly sure that those who felt like a good gossip would repair to the Great House to do just that.

As they were leaving, Hugh had shaken his hand warmly and said, 'Good luck, old man,' and there had been the suspicion of a wink about his eye. Nick, feeling young and light-hearted, had done the very unvicarish thing of winking back. He had turned to Miss Quinn, who was putting on an amazingly stylish jacket.

'Must you go, Patsy?'

'I promised to pop in on Granny. She's expecting me for the weekend.'

'So am I.'

'What?'

'Hoping you'll spend some time with me.'

'Why? Do you fancy me?'

'More than I've ever fancied anyone in all my life.'

Patsy eyed him closely. 'You're not a virgin, are you?'

'No, I'm afraid not.'

'Oh, good. That's one less thing I have to worry about.'

'And the others are?'

'Seducing a man of the cloth.'

'Are you going to?' Nick asked.

'Oh, yes,' answered Patsy with feeling and put her arms around his neck.

'How wonderful,' Nick replied, and just stood there while she took the first steps.

It was during the night that Nick noticed a small drop of blood on his duvet and realized that the cat had crept up and was sleeping on his bed. At that moment William, who had been particularly active that night, gave a loud knock on his bedroom door as if to alert him to trouble.

'Thanks, Bill,' Nick shouted jestingly.

Then he saw that Radetsky's ear was cut, not jaggedly but a neat nick. Investigating it, the vicar thought it was not bad enough for the vet but could certainly do with some antiseptic. Putting on his dressing gown and slippers, he called the cat downstairs.

As he bathed the ear with lint and a weak mixture of Dettol and water, he was concentrating on his pet. But his thoughts kept slipping sideways to his other one, his pet girl, the adorable Patsy. She hadn't spent the night and Nick hadn't pushed for it, not from any sense of morality but because he preferred to wait until she was good and ready – or perhaps bad and ready might have been a more apt phrase. He was happy knowing that she was interested in him – very – and waited with a delicious thrill of excitement to see what joys the future would hold. Meanwhile he had done all that he could for the cat and decided to head back to bed, letting Radetsky join him for a special treat. But though he dropped off to sleep again he had bad dreams.

He stood outside a large oak door, bathed in moonlight, the moonlit door. He knocked on it and it swung open slowly to reveal a vivid pastoral scene. There was a gaily painted maypole and children in rustic clothes dancing merrily round it, their ribbons weaving and plaiting into a sparkling display of colour. And then he looked again and saw that little Billy was standing on a stool in the centre, pushing and thrashing to keep the coloured strips away but slowly becoming enmeshed. Nick tried to run forward to help him but found that he could not move, only stand and stare, an impotent and helpless spectator in that brilliantly moonlit scene.

The maypole faded away and now he was alone in that colourless light. He was walking down a frightening lane, with tall hedges fencing him in on either side. Ahead of him, he could hear Dickie Donkin singing:

> *Only make believe I love you*
> *Only make believe that you love me*
> *Others find peace of mind in pretending*
> *Couldn't you? Couldn't I? Couldn't we?*

It was as if he knew about the burgeoning love affair between Nick and Patsy and was either making fun of or approving it.

> *Make believe our lips are blending*
> *In a phantom kiss or two or three*
> *Might as well make believe I love you*
> *For to tell the truth, I do.*

And then Daft Dickie began to scream in genuine terror and the sound was still ringing in Nick's ears when he woke up, dripping with sweat, and decided that there would be no more sleep for him this night.

It was the job that Dominic Tennant hated the most. The interviewing of a subject that he felt fairly sure was innocent and who, to make matters far, far worse, was not only terrified but autistic into the bargain. The psychiatrist was present and so was a very kindly police constable, who was comfortably built and had a genuine smile. Tennant forced a grin on to his face.

'Well, Dickie, how are you today?'

No answer.

The psychiatrist, Peter Holland, had a try. 'We're not here to hurt you, Dickie. Be sure of that. We're only here to ask a few questions and then we can let you go.'

No answer but a swivel of the head and a furtive glance at Holland.

Tennant's turn again. 'If you could just nod your head, Dickie, to show us that you understand.'

The policewoman said gently, 'My mum always told me to nod my head because it was polite.'

Dickie gave a faint nod.

'Breakthrough,' said Tennant under his breath. Aloud he added, 'Well done, Dickie, you just nod and shake your head at us. All right?'

No response at all.

Tennant cleared his throat. 'I'd like to talk about the night of the murder, if I may. You were in the woods, Dickie, we know that, but afterwards, when everyone had gone away, the moon came out very brightly and you wandered over and saw that Billy was attached to the maypole. Is that correct?'

There was a massive shaking of the head and then quite unexpectedly Dickie burst into a great paroxysm of weeping. He bent his arms to his knees and seemed to roll himself into a ball of misery. Throughout this he sobbed violently and stamped his feet and sighed and moaned.

Tennant looked at the psychiatrist, who shook his head. The interview was terminated. Tennant shut off the recorder and nodded at the police constable to take Dickie back to the cells. Then he turned to his friend and said, 'What the hell do I do now?'

Holland said, in his beautiful calm voice, 'Why don't you let him go, Dominic? Can't he stay in someone's garden hut or something? There must be a kindly person who would keep an eye on him for a few days. And leave him plenty of things to draw and paint with. Let him paint what he can't say. I think you'll find that far more productive than caging him up here. Besides, you'd have to arrest him tomorrow or let him go. You don't think he did those murders, do you?'

Tennant shook his head. 'I think he's capable of murder, if that's what you're asking. There was all that funny business years ago. But these sadistic attacks on children don't seem to be his scene somehow.'

'Then take my tip, let him go and let him paint what he wants to show you.'

'Are you sure he will?'

'You never know where you are with autistic people, but as he seems to like drawing, there's as good a chance as any.'

Once back in his room, Tennant put through a call to Giles, and was pleased with the result. An hour later a relieved Dickie Donkin was being driven up to the sheep farmer's place where he had been offered the loan of a garden shed, some blankets, and an old outdoor loo next door. Indeed, he was so happy that he burst into song, which Tennant found oddly pleasing.

> *I'll sing thee songs of Araby*
> *And tales of fair Cashmere*
> *Wild tales to cheat thee of a sigh*
> *Or charm thee to a tear*
> *And dreams of delight shall on thee break*
> *And rainbow visions rise*
> *And all my soul shall strive to wake*
> *Sweet wonder in thine eyes.*

'Was that one of your Granny's tunes?' asked Tennant, and was rewarded with a happy smile.

Potter was talking to Tennant in the Lakehurst incident room. He was describing the high jinks in the woods and the public copulation, and couldn't resist a grin as he did so.

'Should we do anything about it, sir?'

'There were no underage children involved, were there?'

'It was a bit hard to tell with all those masks on but judging by the bodies, I'd say not.'

'Then let them play. What harm can they do? They go to the woods so it's not being done in full public gaze. I'd advise an eye is kept on them, however.'

'So who's going to do that?'

'You, perhaps?'

'As if I haven't got enough to do.'

'Then tell our constables to have a go. And keep it on a rota. We don't want any of them getting addicted and trying to join in.'

'Why is that idea faintly disgusting?'

'Because you're a prude,' said Tennant, and guffawed loudly.

Fractionally cross, Potter went to his computer and typed vigorously, leaving Tennant to muse over how far they had got. The answer was, not far enough. And he was just gloomily surveying the scene when his mobile went off. It was WPC Monica Jones.

'Sir, can you come over to Susan Richards' house? We had a break-in last night. I didn't catch the bastard who did it but I gave them a run for their money.'

'Why didn't you send for backup at the time?'

'I did. I got two WPCs who had all their work cut out trying to calm a screaming hysterical woman and her wretched little son. I went chasing after him.'

Ten minutes later Tennant was talking to Monica in person.

'Tell me exactly what happened.'

'Well, I was sleeping in the guest room, which is at the back of the house, overlooking the garden. About one o'clock I was woken up by a faint scratching sound and I realized that it was somebody at the back door. I crept down the stairs and saw that somebody had got a string on the door key and was trying to pull it under the door.'

'Is there a gap?'

'A very small one. I doubt that they would have managed it. Be that as it may, I stood there in silence and suddenly flung the door open wide. But he must have heard me because they were taking off across the garden like a blasted greyhound. I followed them but it was useless. They must have been trained to run because whoever it was, positively fled.'

'You said "he" when you described them earlier. What makes you think it was a man?'

'I don't know why I said that. I'm sorry.'

Tennant was silent for a long time, then finally said, 'What visitors came to the house yesterday?'

'Several people, all women coming to pay their sympathies.'

'Did any of them have children with them?'

'Several. Why?'

'Because that trick of putting the string on the key must have been done from inside. You think about it. There's no hand small enough to squeeze through a crack and loop it on.'

'You're right. In that case, do you think it was Jonathan himself?'

'No, because it wasn't him you chased through the garden. He was howling inside the house.'

Monica's greyish eyes looked confused. 'It's like a kid's trick and there must have been a good few children here trying to cheer Johnnie up.'

'Names?'

'I'll have to go into my notebook and see exactly who called.'

'While you're doing that I think I'll follow your tracks from last night and see if I can spot anything.'

'OK, Guv,' and she smiled at him and went back into the house.

Tennant went out into the garden and in broad daylight searched the path that Monica must have taken last night. All he could think of as he retraced her steps was that the miscreant must have been small. His mind ran over the small people they had questioned: Reg Varney, the archer, Miss Dunkley the teacher – sounded like a game of Happy Families, he thought absently – Mrs Richards, the dead child's mother. Dominic came to an abrupt halt as he saw the place where the miscreant had run through the hedge. No point going any further than that. He could see the trail leading away to the road where it would become lost. Making a mental note that he must have a long chat with Miss Dunkley, the inspector turned back to the house. And was just about to go back in when he spotted something lying on the ground. It was a broken piece of string, looking trodden on and dirty, like a dead worm, abandoned on the ground. To one end of it was fastened an elastic band. In an instant Tennant saw through it. It had led from the door key, still in the lock, then some young kid had attached it to its wrist. But the scheme had gone horribly wrong and the string had snapped of its own accord. It had been abandoned and thrown away, there and then.

'Any luck?' asked Monica Jones.

'Only this.'

She took it from him and examined it.

'So that is how the little devil was going to get the key out.'

'In their dreams. Any string would snap with that amount of pressure on it.'

'I'd better stay awake all night. It looks to me as if these ruddy kids are all in collusion.'

Tennant went in and knocked gently on Mrs Richards' door. She was holding a glass of martini and looked decidedly sloshed.

'Looks as if you had quite a party this morning,' he said cheerfully. 'Well, a drink never harmed anyone, I say.'

'But it's going to be the bloody waking up that I dread,' she answered, a slur in her voice. 'I'll feel like hell again – and then it will begin all over again, each day a little more ghastly than the last. To know that I have lost my little girl and that she will never be coming back . . .' She sloshed some more martini into her glass and drank it down in one gulp. 'Would you like one, Inspector?'

'No, thanks, I'm on duty. Do you mind if I have the briefest chat with Jonathan?'

'No, where is he?'

'Watching television.'

'Help yourself. You'll probably terrify the life out of him, but what the hell.'

Jonathan was watching an old film with John Wayne, looking somewhat overweight, wearing a Stetson and holding forth about cattle drives. The little boy was looking at it with a glazed expression, clearly not taking in a word.

'Hello, Johnnie,' said Tennant quietly.

He might as well have screamed, for the child leapt with fright and almost immediately started to weep. The door opened and WPC Jones appeared and stood silently in the entrance.

'How are things going?' the inspector asked. For answer Johnnie threw himself on the floor and wept into the carpet. Monica Jones marched forward and picked him up again.

'Now, Johnnie, darling, do stop it. The inspector's here to ask a few questions, that's all. He's trying to catch that nasty person who killed Bobby and Debbie – and I'm sure you'd like to help.'

The child went red in the face and beat against Monica Jones's admirable chest with miniature flying fists.

'Kill me,' he screamed. 'Kill me.'

'Who's going to kill you?' the inspector shouted over the mayhem.

'I can't tell,' sobbed the wretched child and proceeded to have hysterics.

His mother wove into the room. 'What's all this racket? Johnnie, stop it. D'you hear me?' and she gave her son a stinging blow across the face. Though the inspector and the WPC watched in horror, it had the desired effect. He became very quiet and very still, obviously in a state of shock. There was an awkward silence, then eventually the inspector spoke.

'I'll come back another time,' he said. 'If I were you I would ring the doctors' surgery, Mrs Richards. The boy needs medical attention, in my opinion. Something has frightened him out of his wits.'

Susan Richards, awash with martini, scarlet in the face, rivulets of tears of despair, said, 'I wish I were dead and that it was over.'

Monica crossed over to her and took her in her arms. 'Now, we'll have no more of this. You may have lost a daughter but you still have a son, a terrified little boy, who you must love and care for and cherish despite all your grief.'

Dominic Tennant, thinking that the policewoman was ripe for promotion, quietly crept away.

NINETEEN

D aft Dickie was happy for two weeks. During the light hours he painted like a man possessed, pouring out all his anger at the world, every detail that he had seen of the murder, the demon sitting on his chest and how he had thrown it off, the plucking of the arrow out of the strange lump that he had thought to be a chrysalis. Everything that had ever happened to him with one notable exception. He had never and would never paint the death of his stepfather. Other than that, he painted everything that came into his head. And when he got bored with those little stories, he painted the view from Giles's sheep fields, the lambs frisking, the flowers, the trees, even a portrait of Giles himself.

He painted very much in the style of van Gogh, striking colours and faces that you feel you know. He was a primitive of the best kind and yet had never had a painting lesson in his life. But while the mood was upon him he would sit before an easel with brushes and a palette that Giles had managed to rustle up from a local artist who had unfortunately died of booze, and daub away for days. Giles usually invited him in to share the farmhouse supper, then they would sup ale and sing songs of the old days until it was time for Dickie to shamble off to his hut.

But one day when the sheep farmer went looking for his convivial guest, he had gone. Just like a shadow, he had slipped out one night and not returned. After pondering the fact for most of the morning, Giles had put through a call to Inspector Tennant, who had said, 'I'll pop up and see you, Giles, when I've got a spare minute.'

Because all hell had broken out in Lewes. They had received an email from another constabulary telling them of a local coven which had used children in their rituals, one of whom had subsequently died. Even though this had taken place some years ago it was still a lead that needed following up. He and Potter had found themselves heading for Exeter at a time when they could well have done with staying at home. Nothing at all had broken in the murder case near Lakehurst, and despite looking through endless reports, diligent house-to-house enquiries, and a great deal of questioning, the inspector and Potter were almost at exactly the same point as when they started making enquiries.

It had been a fortnight now and much had changed. Olivia had left for her flat in Chiswick as she was now rehearsing in the mornings at a studio in London, and though she had offered the cottage to Tennant, he had refused and returned to his own apartment in Lewes. And then Superintendent Miller had received personal information about the coven in Devon, and Potter was hitting the motorway faster than a dose of Epsom salts.

'I don't think I can manage this twice in one day, sir.'

'I don't expect you to. I've booked us rooms for the night in Sidmouth in one of those glorious hotels along the front. They're Victorian and some of them are still run on the same lines. A gong is struck for dinner and five minutes before it one can hear the elderly residents rustling behind their doors waiting for the sound.'

'You don't mean it.'

'I do.'

'What happens next?'

'At the first beat of the gong bedroom doors fly open and they make a dash, knocking each other aside with Zimmer frames and walking sticks to be first in the dining room.'

'Have they got selected tables?'

'Oh, yes, the residents have. The guests are put by the window where they can see the sea.'

'It doesn't sound a bit like you, Dominic.'

'Ah, it reminds me of my ignoble youth when I used to sprint down the stairs, past the disorderly crocodile, and be the first in.'

'How very unkind.'

'It was. But then I was only sixteen years old and on a cycling holiday. We stayed in Sidmouth three glorious days. Put the whole episode down to a ghoulish sense of fun.'

'I don't think I will look at you in quite the same way again, Inspector.'

As luck would have it the interview in Exeter was relatively short. The bare facts were that there was a dark coven functioning in an out-of-the-way hamlet called Combe St Mary, who had kidnapped local children and then subjected them to horrifying ordeals. One of the children had died of fright and the police had moved in and broken the ring up and the chief wizard had gone down for a good stretch, as had several other of the gang members. It was similar in a way but not quite near enough to the Lakehurst situation, thought Potter, recalling the bouncing bottoms and dangling doodahs. That had just been an excuse for public sex. The Devon crew had had much nastier intentions. Tennant and Potter had come away with a great deal of paper, effusive thanks but little else. Then they had made their way to the Seymour Hotel.

It was very much as Potter had expected, its exterior painted a liverish yellow, with a weary sign reading 'Seymour Hot', the rest having blown down in some storm or other. There was a clanking old lift with doors that one had to pull across, which eventually deposited the two policemen on the third floor. Tennant had a sea view, which completely made up for the room's some-what bare essentials, but Potter was at the back, overlooking a car park and a line of miserable waste bins overflowing with detritus the seagulls were attacking with cries of jubilation.

They deliberately walked down before the gong when it came to dinner time and had the amusing experience of hearing the patrons trembling with excitement as gong time drew near. But as the charge to dine was declared and the multitude made for the stairs, Tennant took his sergeant firmly by the elbow and propelled him out of the building and along the seafront to another hotel where they had a reasonably decent meal. It was still light when they came out – they ate early in Sidmouth – and the sea was completely calm, meeting the sky with an almost invisible line.

'God, the air's like wine,' said Potter, taking large breaths in. 'Let's go for a bit of a walk. Do us good.'

They walked along the front to the very end of the promenade, beyond which more cottages were built on a slight incline. They ascended the small hill and then the inspector stopped dead in front of an attractive period building.

'Well, I never knew that,' he said.

Staring, Potter read a small blue plaque. 'Constance Kent was born and lived here,' he read aloud. 'That's the child murderer, isn't it?'

'Yes, it is. I just can't imagine her coming into the world in such beautiful surroundings. You would think it would wash the soul clean for all eternity.'

'Instead she stabbed her four-year-old half-brother, cut his throat and threw him into the shit in the privy.'

'That's the one.' Tennant turned to face Potter. 'Do you think people are born with an evil streak? Or do you think it develops because they had a raw deal along the way?'

'Both, sir.'

'Then you truly believe that Constance Kent and all the other individuals like her have some inner perversion that makes them enjoy inflicting pain?'

'Yes, I suppose I do.' Potter shivered. 'Come on, Dominic, it's getting chilly. Let's go and have a drink.'

'Race you to The Marine. Last one in buys the drinks.'

And they set off like a couple of school kids heading for the ice cream parlour.

School had resumed and Miss Dunkley was delighted to have something to take the children's minds off the recent murders. His name was Byron Wheeler and he was hardly the most prepossessing child one could imagine. He was overweight, not very tall, but his redeeming features were his eyes and hair. Both were dark and vivid. His father had started in house clearance but in that amazing East End way had turned himself into an antique dealer and eventually a celebrity who appeared on *Antiques For All*. He had loads of money, as the saying went, and had just bought himself a house near Lakehurst, complete with swimming pool and an outdoor bar. His name was Tommy Wheeler and his nickname, Wheeler the Dealer.

Byron was greeted with a certain amount of suspicion but when one of the boys had called him a poof, he had flattened the accuser with a swipe of his knuckles. After this incident he was treated with caution and respect. But his chubby personality had won the heart of little Miss Goldilocks, Isabelle Wyatt herself, and he was duly invited to tea.

Byron's mother, a skinny blonde who wore a great deal of

make-up and kept her figure by only eating courgettes, had lectured him on how to behave.

'Don't just grab a cake, Byron, wait until one is offered and then say, "I think I have a little room left," and take it nicely.'

'How do you do that, Mum?'

'Oh, I don't know. Between your thumb and your first finger. Or something. Ask your dad.'

But Tommy had just laughed and said, 'Be yourself, son. They're only asking you 'cos I'm on the telly.'

So with his head full of these rather mixed messages, Byron had been driven by his mother in a white people carrier with blacked-out windows. Melissa had come out to meet him, glad with all her heart that her granddaughter had at last stopped weeping hysterically and asked a child to tea. She was somewhat taken aback as Byron's stocky form emerged from the ostentatious transport in which he had been conveyed. Much to her consternation, he bowed, then stuck his hand out and said, 'How do you do, my lady?'

Melissa smiled at him. 'Hello, Byron, how are you?'

'I am very well, thank you,' he answered in an Eliza Doolittle-elocuted voice.

Isabelle came up, her golden hair swinging behind her. At a short distance followed Hugh, his expression thoughtful.

'How kind of you to let me come,' said Byron, bowing.

Hugh smiled. 'The pleasure is mine, Byron. And you can just be yourself here. We don't expect anything in the way of high-falutin talk.'

Byron smiled faintly. 'Oh, I see.' But he didn't.

He and Isabelle romped off into the depths of the garden. Hugh, watching them, said, 'She seems to have quite recovered from that horrible business with Billy.'

'Yes, poor little girl. It really affected her badly. And the murder of Debbie practically destroyed her.'

'I think you were the one who suffered most, my darling.'

'Hugh, who do you think was responsible for those sadistic deaths?'

'My money would be on that devil worshipper, O'Hare. Either him or that little archery guy, Reg Marney.'

'Why do you say that?'

'Because they are the only two who fit the bill. Unless . . .'

'Unless what?'

'Nothing. Just a silly thought of mine. Come on, let's go and make tea for Belle's new friend. What do you think of him, by the way?'

'I thought he was terribly sweet. Trying desperately hard to be refined.'

'He's just a poor little blighter that will be sent for elocution lessons when all he wants to do is what suits him, talk Cockney.'

'Like his father. He's Tommy Wheeler.'

'Who?'

'Oh, Hugh, he's one of the experts on *Antiques For All*. He's got a great personality, the original East Ender. You're always asleep behind your newspaper by the time he comes on.'

'That's not the show with that awful woman presenter, is it?'

'Yes. Thinks the sun shines out of her bottom. I can't stand her but I do love it when they discover that the jug that some old couple have been using to keep flowers in is actually twelfth-century Ming.'

Hugh laughed and gave her a playful smack on the behind and they went into the house arm in arm.

O'Hare and Marney were working on a rather wonderful car which belonged to the Russian princess who lived up in the castle with Sir Rufus Beaudegrave. They had never been told formally that she was a princess but they knew a class act when they saw one and had drawn their own conclusions. The car had been hoisted up on a lift and the two men were jointly examining its braking system.

'Wish I could fix this so that she broke down in the woods and got drawn into a coven meeting,' said Reg, smacking his lips.

'I've told you a thousand times that it's too dangerous to meet at the moment. I know that one of those policemen saw us. He looked straight at me.'

'Perhaps he wanted to join in.'

'Some hopes. Anyway, the place is still crawling with 'em. And it won't stop till they've caught whoever did it. Do you hear me, Reg?'

Marney rose to his full five foot two inches. 'Are you pointing the finger?'

'Those crimes have got your handprints all over them. The low arrow shot, your love of little children. Come on, Reg, you did them. Admit it.'

Reg slanted his eyes. 'I was thinking just the same about you, Chris. Why don't you tell me the truth? I know what you look at on your computer.'

O'Hare suddenly picked up a wrench. 'Don't you dare say those things aloud. One more word out of you and you'll get this over your head.'

'All right, all right, keep your shirt on. I know you're constantly on the lookout for children of Mr Grimm, Chris. Let's leave it like that, shall we?'

For answer Chris picked him up by the scruff of his neck and shook the little man violently.

'Not another word, d'you hear? What I know, I know. And it's best left like that.'

Reg was gasping for breath as he settled himself back on to his feet. At that moment he hated the Devil's man with every bone in his small body. But it was a good job in the garage and life was hard. Best to bide his time and wait until something better came along. And if Chris were mad enough to try and conjure up the Devil and his minions, then so be it. He would keep his mouth closed.

The case was going cold, Tennant felt sure of it. And yet he had a nagging feeling that the answer lay there just below the surface, if only he had the ability to pull it to the forefront of his brain. On an impulse he parked his car in the High Street and knocked on the door of the vicarage. Nick answered, looking just as a young vicar in a rural community should look: fresh-faced and keen, yet with the sorrows and mysteries of the whole locality thrust upon him.

'Inspector Tennant – Dominic – how very nice to see you. Come in, come in.'

The policeman walked into Nick's living room to see Radetsky, the cat, lying on the sofa looking at the world from a mournful eye.

'Hello, what's up with your moggie? He looks miserable.'

'Yes, he's on antibiotics. I had to take him to the vet's. He had a cut in his ear which went septic. Must have caught it on something.'

'Poor pussy.' Tennant gave him a tentative tickle. 'Well, how are you, Nick? It's been quite a while since we spoke.'

'Oh, I'm jogging along, you know. But I wish this wretched case could draw to a conclusion. It's upset a lot of people in the village.'

'You're telling me. Nobody wants it as much as I do.'

'Are you any further on?'

'Not really.' Tennant accepted the glass of gin and tonic that Nick was offering him. 'But I have a strange feeling that it's all connected with devil worship. There's so much of it goes on in rural Sussex. Mr Grimm casts a long shadow.'

The vicar pulled a face. 'I know. And it's my duty to fight it to the bitter end. I feel sometimes that it is a battle I can't win.'

'Oh come, Nick, don't say that. It's part of the old Christian ethic that good will triumph over evil.'

'But when you're on the front line it doesn't always feel that way.'

Tennant sipped his gin and said, 'I see you as St George, carrying your flaming sword and standing before the moonlit door to repel all evildoers.'

Nick rolled his eyes. 'Are you misquoting de la Mare to annoy me?'

Tennant shook his head. 'One of our greatest poets and one who is sadly overlooked, I fear. "The Listeners" is my favourite poem of all time.'

'What I love about it was that it was never explained, not even by the author. I mean, what is it about?'

'"Is there anybody there?" said the Traveller, knocking on the moonlit door,' quoted Tennant. He shook his head. 'I think it just tells the story of a creepy old house bathed in moonlight, and somebody from their past comes as he says he would, but everybody he once knew has died.'

'Yes, that's about it in my opinion too.'

'Then I propose a toast. To the late, great Walter de la Mare.'

They clinked glasses and solemnly drank.

'You know we're a couple of idiots quoting poetry at each other when I've got the most awful couple of murders to solve. And you seem to be fighting off some takeover bid by the devil worshippers.'

'Perhaps it was the only way to lift our spirits,' Nick answered gloomily.

'I take it from your general disposition that you have not seen Miss Quinn lately.'

Nick's features lifted. 'Do you know, I have seen her and quite honestly I've really fallen for her. I just wish she were more available to court. That sounds old-fashioned, doesn't it? But then I suppose I'm just an old-fashioned chap. I would take her out to dinner and buy her flowers and dance the night away if she only lived nearer.'

'Where does she live?'

'Her parents are divorced and her mother lives in Budleigh Salterton. Her father pushed off and lives in Croynge or Penge or Windge East. The only hope is her grandmother who, thankfully, lives in the village.'

'But Patsy's tour can't last forever. I mean, she only came fifth in that contest.'

'I know,' Nick answered miserably, 'but she'll always be a singer.'

'Get a grip, Vicar. Nowadays women invariably have a profession. Tell me, are your intentions matrimonial?'

'They may well lean in that direction, yes.'

'Well, I'm pleased to hear it. Whether she'll want you is an entirely different matter, of course. But if I were you, Nick, I would go and sweet-talk her granny, be kind to the old dear and take her little gifts. It certainly can't do any harm if it doesn't do any good.'

'You're right,' said Nick. 'I shall start tomorrow. And I'll probably end up by marrying the grandmother instead.'

'Quite likely,' answered Tennant, and they both laughed.

Byron wasn't enjoying his tea with Isabelle one little bit. She had dared him to swim in their swimming pool – which lay at the very far end of the garden – and stared at him when he had refused.

'But I 'aven't brought my trunks. I can't swim in me pants.'

'Yes, you can, sissy. I can go in in my knickers. I don't think you can swim.'

'I can so. My dad says I'm a very good swimmer.'

But Belle had persisted and in the end the boy, rather ashamed because he had little rolls of fat about his person, had stripped to his underpants and dived in. He was, as his father had claimed, an excellent swimmer. Doing a long, leisurely crawl up and down the length of the pool and producing just a small rivulet of crystal drops, not great waves of heaving water like the creatures in goggles who scare old ladies at the baths in health clubs.

Isabelle jumped in but she could only do the breast stroke and felt puny in comparison with the rippling motion of Byron.

'Who taught you to swim like that?' she asked pettishly, as Byron came to a stop beside her.

'I've had lessons since I was five. Me and Dad belong to a posh health club and I was taught there.'

'You're a show-off, that's what you are, Byron Wheeler.'

'I'm not, honest. I've just been taught right.'

Belle let out a shriek of rather nasty laughter. In fact, it made Byron – who was not the most imaginative of children – go cold.

'Well, go on swimming. Show me how it's done. I'll go and watch you.'

Obediently, for Byron was really a nice little boy who did what he was told, he started to swim again He did the crawl superbly, just to show her, head under the water, coming up to take a puff, until he suddenly realized that it was getting dark and the next thing he knew was that the pool cover was unrolling on top of him. Frantically he swam towards the light but she was too quick for him. She had unrolled the whole top and he was trapped beneath. He couldn't even get his head up to shout and Byron realized that he was dying.

And then he heard a voice, loud and authoritative. 'Isabelle, what the hell do you think you're doing? Where's Byron?'

'Oh, he's gone home, Daddy. Wasn't it rude of him?'

Byron feebly raised an arm and the top must have rippled slightly because he heard the major shout, 'He's under there. Go and fetch your mother. I'll deal with you later.' And the major started heaving on the wheel with every ounce of his power.

Melissa came running and the two of them hauled with all their strength but Byron had lost consciousness by the time the cover was off and it was only because the major had brought soldiers back from the brink of death that the child was still alive when they took him into the ambulance.

'Oh God, Hugh, could that have been an accident?'

'No,' he answered shortly, 'no it couldn't. Isabelle must have done it for a prank. But that is the kindest way of looking at it. I'm going to have words with that young lady. Where is she?'

'In her room. I sent her upstairs.'

But she wasn't there. She wasn't anywhere in the house. And to make matters worse the cat, Samba, who had spent most of his time in his basket since returning from surgery at the vets, was missing too.

Hugh had sat quietly, just for a few minutes, gathering his strength as if he were donning army uniform. Then he said, 'I'm going to find her, Melissa.'

'I'm coming with you, darling.'

'Only if you promise me that you will return home once darkness falls.'

'Once darkness falls,' repeated Melissa, and there was fear in her voice.

TWENTY

Dickie had found his wandering footsteps turning towards Foxfield without any instruction from himself. Whether it was because he missed company – and the most congenial company he had ever found had been round Lakehurst and its environs – he did not know. His brain was not capable of working such things out. He burst into song as he glimpsed the distant lights of The White Hart.

> *I'm only a strolling vagabond*
> *So goodnight pretty maiden, goodnight.*
> *I'm bound for the hills and the valleys beyond,*
> *So goodnight pretty maiden, goodnight.*

He tried for the next line but found he could not remember it. Besides, he was getting near houses. It would not be good for them to know he was round about. For no reason other than a strong feeling of self-preservation, Dickie began to slow down. He could hear voices coming through one of the open cottage windows.

'I'm sorry, Mr O'Hare, to call on you like this but I felt so frightened. I was only playing a prank on my friend but my daddy threatened to smack my bottom.'

Dickie strained his ears to hear the reply.

'There, there, my dear. We all play pranks from time to time. I bet you your mother did.'

'What do you mean? My real mother is dead. I never knew her.'

'I have a feeling that your real mother was a handmaiden of Mr Grimm.'

There was a pause as if Belle was trying to work out what to say, then she answered, 'I truly don't know. I could never ask her because she was killed before I could talk.'

'That would be his way, of course. Do you bear your father's mark?'

'What do you mean?'

'Have you a mole or a port wine stain on your body?'

'I have a mole on my heart. Is it important?'

'Very. Will you show it to me? You see, it could be your father's way of picking you out.'

There was a silence and then Belle said, 'I feel excited. And wicked. I feel like I've never felt before.'

Dickie would have crept up to the window then to see what was going on but two people came walking down the lane, chatting, and by instinct he hid in the hedge. When he re-emerged all the lights had gone out in Chris O'Hare's cottage and he was left to wonder exactly what had taken place next.

The first thing that Hugh Wyatt had done before he left the house was to phone the police using the card that bore Inspector Tennant's number on it. He had not been put directly through but he explained to the officer that there had been an accident at his house and that his daughter had been involved. Then he had rung off, abruptly, before they could ask him any questions. He had followed Melissa out through the front door, looking at the place where Samba's travelling basket had once stood, wondering why on earth the child should have taken the cat with her.

As if she had heard his thoughts, Melissa said, 'She always adored Samba, of course, poor little darling.'

'You think that's why she took him?'

'Of course. Why else?'

'I don't know why, Melissa.'

And glancing up at him his wife saw that his face was set in the hard lines that she remembered seeing when he first came back from Afghanistan.

It was the low cry of pain that first drew Reg Marney's eye down to the floor of The White Hart in Foxfield. He could see nothing but a trail of blood leading from the door to behind the bar and his stomach gave a strange twist. Despite his penchant for dancing naked and outdoor copulation, Reg had a strange dislike of seeing blood and to have been a donor would have reduced him to near hysteria. Despite his natural dislike he steeled himself and looked behind the bar.

There was a cat in extremis. There was no other phrase to describe its condition. The poor creature was covered with little stab wounds and its short, stubby tail had been the victim of someone with a warped sense of humour because it had been tied tightly round with a red ribbon, the same colour as its disappearing blood.

'My God,' said Reg. 'Help. There's a dying cat in here.'

A man he had seen before in the Great House and recognized as one of Lakehurst's doctors, pushed his way forward.

'Where?' he asked, his accent slightly foreign.

'Down there,' said Reg, indicating with his foot.

Without hesitation Dr Rudniski plunged his hands into the midst of the blood and picked the wretched animal up. He turned to Reg.

'Ring the vet and tell him I'm bringing in a badly wounded cat. Tell him it's very urgent. Oh, and by the way, tell him I'm Kasper.'

'Right,' said Reg, and pulled his mobile out of his pocket.

Charlie, the landlord, sailed up in all his magnificence. 'What's going on?'

'A cat was bleeding to death behind your bar. The Lakehurst doctor, the Polish one, is taking it to the vet's. I don't know if it'll pull through.'

'It's made a right mess. I shouldn't think it's got a drop of blood left in it.'

'Well, go and wash this filthy witness,' said Reg, quoting Macbeth.

'Don't you tell me what to do,' answered Charlie, irate.

'I think I'll just finish my beer and leave.'

The vet, a middle-aged man, with a smile he kept for the owners of his patients and which left his face punctually at six o'clock, looked bleakly at Kasper.

'Whatever bastard did this to the poor animal?'

Kasper shook his head, suddenly sick of the world. 'God knows. I can't imagine anyone doing such a thing to hurt an innocent creature. The whole idea revolts me.'

'Well, it's not in pain now. I've given the poor beast an injection.'

'You mean you've put it down?'

'No. I'm going to operate tonight. I'll call one of the nurses in. I'm going to fight for it to stay alive. By the way, I think you know the owners,' said the vet.

'I probably do. Who are they?'

'They're called Wyatt and live at that large house with the pool just outside the village. Their wretched cat has had its share of suffering, I can tell you. Somebody slashed its tail off the other week.'

'What?'

'Yes, and it was no accident. It was severed with a knife.'

'This story gets more hideous. By the way, I went to see their child. She became quite hysterical after the murders of her friends.'

'Funny little girl, isn't she? My Molly went there to tea once but refused to go again or even to have Isabelle back. She never said why. Strange.'

'Very. Look, Malcolm, I've got to go. Keep in touch about the cat, will you.'

'I'll have more news in the morning.'

'Thanks. I'll give you a ring.'

Kasper got into his car, his mind seething with all the thoughts going through it. Driving back, too fast, he parked in the High Street, and went straight to the vicarage. Nick didn't answer his bell and Kasper hurried to the Great House to see the vicar tucked cosily in a corner with that golden girl, Miss Quinn. Putting aside everything he had thought of asking, Kasper gave them a pleasant wave and ordered himself a vodka, knowing that he would have to get quite inebriated before he could sleep on what he thought he knew.

Tennant received the message that a Major Hugh Wyatt had phoned him about an accident involving his daughter and had then broken off the call and had not answered his phone when the police rang back. Locating Potter quickly, driving in his innocent way back to Lewes, Tennant got in beside his unprotesting young sergeant, who obediently turned the car round.

'Time you got yourself a girlfriend, Mark. You're such an obliging bloke.'

'Well, I've had one or two, sir. Why do you ask?'

'I don't know. Just that life can be a bit lonely sometimes.'

'Do you think it's time I settled down?'

'Yes, frankly. You're such a nice young fellow and I believe some girl would be really lucky to have you.'

'I'll think about it. Anyway, what's the trouble with the Wyatts?'

'I don't know. Major Wyatt put through a call earlier, muttering something about an accident involving his daughter. Then rang off. Meanwhile we've received a call from Tommy Wheeler, the antique dealer, as he likes to call himself.'

'Do you mean the one on *Antiques For All*?'

'Yes, the man himself. He's complaining about his son being half killed up at the Wyatts' house. Apparently the boy was hospitalized.'

'What!'

'Yes, you heard correctly. There's something extremely rum about the whole business. So we're currently hunting Major Wyatt.'

'I don't completely trust him. Do you think we should phone for backup?'

'Steady on, Mark. You've been watching too many American movies. This is just a nice social call to enquire about dear little Isabelle.'

Mark raised a quizzical eyebrow but said nothing and they drove up to the house in silence, each man thinking his own thoughts.

The place was deserted, empty, not a chink of light showing anywhere.

'Let's have a look round while it's still light,' said Tennant. They walked the length of the considerable garden and saw the pool with the cover firmly closed. Then they walked back to the deserted house. The light was just beginning to fade and the trees of the forest, which crept up to the house's very edge like an enemy advancing inch by inch, were beginning to darken.

'I'm glad I don't live here,' said Mark over his shoulder, shivering.

'Why? I think it's a pleasant location. My idea of a dream house.'

At that moment a vixen, very near at hand, let out an unearthly howl, making both of them stop in their tracks.

'It sounds just like a mother screaming for her lost baby.'

'Probably what Melissa Wyatt is doing at this very moment.'

'That's not funny, sir.'

'No, it isn't. You're quite right. I feel a chat with the vicar is necessary. He's always a fount of village gossip. And perhaps he can cure me of this nasty habit of saying the wrong thing. Anyway it's just possible that the Wyatts have ended up in Lakehurst with the wretched child.'

'And I am sure you could do with a pint,' said Mark, a touch of acidity belied by his charming smile.

The Great House was reasonably full but not so packed as to stop Dominic noticing two things as soon as he entered. The first was the vicar, sitting opposite the lovely Miss Quinn and appearing so enchanted, so completely under her beautiful spell, that it seemed cruel to interrupt him. The second was Dr Kasper Rudniski, looking terribly depressed and staring into his glass of vodka as if he would like to wring its neck. The decision was not difficult.

'Good evening, Doctor,' said Tennant, somewhat over-heartily. 'Do you mind if the sergeant and I join you?'

Kasper, remembering his manners, stood up and made a small bow. 'No, please do. I am sorry. I was deep in thought.'

'Any particular reason?'

'Actually, I was worried about a cat.'

'A cat!' exclaimed Potter.

'Yes. It's a cat belonging to the Wyatts. It's black, called Samba. Well, it crawled into The White Hart – God knows what it was doing out at Foxfield – horribly injured.' He paused and drank his glass down rapidly. Tennant signalled with his eyes for Potter to go to refill it.

'Carry on.'

'Well, it had been stabbed a dozen or so times. It was hiding behind the bar and, to be honest, it was dying. I picked it up and drove it straight to Malcolm Martin, the vet. He was closed but he opened up for me. And that's the end of the story, actually.'

'Did it die?' asked Potter, returning with a full glass which Kasper accepted appreciatively.

'I don't know. He was due to operate on it tonight. He was so disgusted by the sight that he said he was going to do his best to save it.'

Tennant sat back in his chair, feeling his brain going into overdrive. Who else had had an injured cat recently? Could there be a connection? And as the thread grew and began to form a web, he actually paled at the prospect before him. Without a word to anyone he rose from his place and crossed the floor to where the vicar and Patsy sat in a rose-coloured bower of their mutual admiration.

'Excuse me interrupting, Vicar, Miss Quinn, but I have something rather important to ask you?'

Nick came back down to earth and it was a difficult descent. His village persona slowly emerged and his cordial smile appeared.

'Good evening, Inspector. How can I help you?'

'I'll come straight to the point. Can you remember what day of the week it was when your cat's ear was injured?'

Miss Quinn's golden eyebrows lifted and the vicar looked puzzled.

'Let me see now. It was a Wednesday, I think. Yes, it was. There was a meeting of the friends of the church – that is the official title of the fundraisers. They don't have to be churchgoers, just people interested in preserving the old building. Why?'

'Could you tell me the names of everyone who came, please?'

'Is it important?'

'It could be. Very.'

'Well, there was Mrs Ivy Bagshot, Mavis, one of my church wardens, Mr and Mrs Honeywell, Mr and Mrs Burton and Major and Mrs Wyatt. It's only a small, informal group.'

'Did the Wyatts have their granddaughter with them?'

'Yes, now you come to mention it, they did. She sat in the living room and watched television.'

'Was she alone?'

'Yes, quite. Except for – the cat.' The vicar's voice trailed away. 'But she couldn't have hurt it. That wound was made with something sharp. There was nothing . . .'

'Do you mind if we go and have a look?'

'But the room has been cleaned – twice. It was over a week ago.'

'All the same. Just to put my mind at rest.'

The enchanted moment between the couple had vanished. Miss Quinn said stiffly, 'Well, I'll only get in the way. I'll be at Granny's if you want me, Nick.'

'Thank you, Patsy. I'll phone you later, if that's all right.'

'Of course,' she answered.

He watched her go out of the door with such a sad expression that, despite everything, the inspector smiled.

'Come along, Vicar, as they used to say long ago. We'll only have a quick look round and then we'll be on our way.'

'But what exactly are you searching for?'

'Something sharp that would cut a cat's ear.'

Nick Lawrence's face grew a shade paler. 'Do you mean Radetsky was attacked?'

The inspector looked official. 'I can't comment on that, I'm afraid. We're just following a line of enquiry.'

In silence the three men walked briskly to the vicarage and Nick switched on the lights of the living room, then stood and watched while Tennant and Potter began a thorough search of the room, mostly with their eyes, covering their hands with disposable gloves before they touched anything. Eventually, digging behind the books on the shelves by Nick's favourite armchair, Potter cried 'Got something,' and pulled out a pair of scissors.

The vicar stared. 'But they are not kept there. They're usually on my desk.'

Potter held them up to the light. 'There's a small bloodstain on them.'

'Bag them up,' answered the inspector. He looked round. 'Where's the cat now?'

Nick called and Radetsky came in from the kitchen.

'I'd keep him in for the next few days.'

'Are you serious?'

'Never been more so.'

'Very well. I'll do what you say.'

And as Nick showed them out into the darkness he felt a great unease, a mighty chill, as if the forces of evil had combined in someone and he must do something about it. He locked the house and crossed the road into the church where he went to have a serious conversation with the Almighty Powerhouse.

'Where to now?' asked Potter as they got into the car.

'I don't know,' Tennant answered wearily. 'Let's have one more look at the Wyatts' house and then . . . I'm not sure.'

It was only a short drive to the outlying home of the major and his wife and this time they saw that the lights were on. At first nobody answered their knocking but Tennant called loudly, 'It's the police, Major. We've just come to check that everything is all right?'

They heard the bolts slide back and then, looking like a ghost, her blonde hair tinted white by the light behind her, Melissa Wyatt answered. As soon as she saw Tennant she burst into tears.

'Oh, it's all so awful,' she said in a voice choking with tears.

'What is?' Tennant asked. 'What is it that's worrying you, Mrs Wyatt?'

'My granddaughter – little Isabelle – has run away and she's taken the cat with her. Well, I presume she has. Because the cat and its basket were both missing when we realized she had gone.'

Potter said, 'Your cat has been found, Mrs Wyatt. It has been seriously injured and at the moment is with Malcolm Martin who is operating on it. I'm afraid that is all I know.'

Her eyes, the colour of wild violets, flashed up at him. 'Poor, poor Samba. Had he been run over?'

Potter shook his head. 'I'm afraid that's all I know.'

'But where did this happen?'

He saw the almost imperceptible shake of Tennant's head.

'I'm sorry, Mrs Wyatt, I've told you everything I can. Just be sure your cat is in the best hands and will be well looked after.'

'Where is your husband?' asked Tennant.

'He's still out searching for Isabelle. You have no news of her?'

'Not as yet, no. But be assured we will find her and bring her back safely.'

'I can't think why she ran away. Of course, her grandfather was very annoyed with her about that silly prank.'

'You mean the one involving the television man's son?'

'Yes. But it wasn't serious, Inspector, it was just foolishness.'

Melissa Wyatt collapsed into another fit of weeping and
Tennant, leaving the room, phoned for the remarkable WPC
Monica Jones to come immediately and sit with the distressed
woman while he and Potter, in typical male fashion, dodged the
issue entirely.

They got back into the car and headed straight back to the
incident room where Tennant put out a general call that a small
girl had run away and every effort must be made to locate her.
Then he turned to Potter.

'I've just got a feeling about this. It was deep in Speckled
Wood that you saw them all prancing about, wasn't it?'

'Yes,' said his sergeant, and giggled aloud at the memory.
'Human flesh can be quite off-putting, can't it?'

'Well, it depends on the circumstances,' answered Tennant,
smiling.

'You're right, of course. But I'll never forget seeing a family
once on a nudist beach. It was the poor young woman who had
me almost hysterical. She was trying to get into a boat and had
one foot on board and one on the mainland. I'll leave the rest to
your vivid imagination.'

'Oh, dear,' said Tennant, laughing in spite of himself.

'It was more a case of split the difference,' answered Potter
and guffawed long and loud to relieve the tension.

They eventually quietened down and headed for Speckled
Wood, parked the car and silently walked to the grove. But tonight
it was empty. There was not a sign of a living soul. Rather disappointed, they made their way back to the car.

'Where now, sir?'

'I think we'll make a brief call on old Giles. He usually knows
everything that's going on.'

The lights in the farmhouse were on and so was the television.
Giles had been sitting comfortably, his dogs asleep at his feet, a
pint of beer at his side, watching – of all things – a film about
Margot Fonteyn.

'I wouldn't have thought you'd have liked that kind of thing,
Giles,' said Tennant as they walked in.

'I love ballet,' he answered. 'I go to Covent Garden whenever
I can afford it.'

'Do you really!' exclaimed Potter in surprise.

'Yes, I do. I enjoy it.'

'I'm a bit of an opera buff myself,' said Tennant.

'Ah, Glyndebourne,' said Giles. 'I've been there and all.'

The conversation was taking such an unusual twist that Tennant decided to drop it. 'Have you seen anything of Daft Dickie recently?' he asked.

'Not recently, no. He lived here quite contentedly for about a fortnight and then one night he just pushed off into the darkness. But I can assure you of this, Inspector, he was a good lad while he was here. Made no trouble for me or anyone else.'

'When I interviewed him in Lewes it was very difficult to get him to talk, so the psychiatrist advised him to paint what he didn't want to talk about. Did he?'

'He did indeed. The hut's bursting with paintings. Come and have a look at them.'

They followed him into the garden and down a winding path to where the hut, sturdy and timbered, stood bathed in moonlight.

'Does it have any electricity?'

'No, just a couple of oil lamps. I'll light them.'

Giles unlocked the door and stepped into the darkness. They heard the striking of a match and then slowly the light from one of the oil lamps lit the scene. Tennant drew breath. A blaze of colour leapt out, dazzling him. A million stars danced before his eyes. There in all the splendour of the work of a true genius he saw slashed across canvas representations which brought him almost to his knees. Nothing could have prepared him for what he was about to find as he entered the shed.

Dickie had not only seen the murders but had painted in swingeing detail graphic images of them. Tennant and Potter stood silently, Potter holding up one lamp, as the brilliance of the scenes were revealed in all their brutal, stark, uncompromising detail. They saw the figure attached to the maypole; they saw the small creature in front, armed with bow and arrow, taking aim, back turned to the viewer. But there, hanging down from her wreath of flowers, was a mass of primrose hair.

'Mr Grimm's daughter,' said Tennant.

'Look at this one, sir.'

Potter was holding up a scene painted in vivid deep blue, a

midnight scene made all the more horrific because two children were in the foreground, one mercilessly beating the other to death.

'Remind you of anything?' said Tennant, his voice suddenly harsh.

'James Bulger, sir. There are children who are thoroughly evil and I'm afraid we've come across another one.'

Tennant sighed heavily. 'I haven't experienced anything like this. Oh, yes, I've had little thieves, little beasts whose parents have given up on them, juvenile delinquents, you name it. But killing for killing's sake? God Almighty. The child must be deranged.'

'Do you remember the sweet face of Mary Bell, sir? She strangled two boys while she was still eleven years old and when she came out from whatever sentence she got, the court granted anonymity for her and her daughter for life.'

'Like James Bulger's killers. Total anonymity.'

The two men stood staring at one another, shaking their heads.

Giles, who had been standing close by, said, 'So Miss Goody Two-Shoes is the guilty party?'

'So it would seem, my friend. But keep this absolutely confidential for the time being. Oh, and Giles . . .'

'Yes?'

'Phone this number tomorrow and say you're ringing on my behalf. It's a well-known art dealer and I want him to come and have a look at these.'

'Do you mean that he might buy them? Will our Dickie be famous one day?'

'There's always a chance. They buy very strange things in the art world.'

And with that the two policemen hurried to their car.

TWENTY-ONE

Alone, under the full moon, Major Hugh Wyatt paused for breath. He felt as if a mighty hand had been laid upon him and he had changed into someone who lay just below the surface, someone with whom he could identify, a primitive hunter, a man who righted wrongs. But even as he felt these things sweep over him, forcefully, enough to make him lose his breath all over again, he had a moment of intense realization. No, he was not any of those things. He was Major Hugh Wyatt who had served in Afghanistan and whose mission it was to see right done.

He straightened up, listening as immediately above his head a bird began to sing. Surely it must be a nightingale, but there weren't any nightingales in Speckled Wood. But then reality and make-believe had become somewhat blurred as he wrestled with the problem of his granddaughter being a monstrous creation, that she tortured people and cats, that she revelled in inflicting pain, that she was depraved and ugly. That she must be cast from the earth and that he was the man whose mission it was to accomplish this.

Hugh suddenly sat down on the ground and wept bitterly. It was no good pretending he was the one who must rid the world of an evil sprite. He had loved her ever since she had been placed in Melissa's arms by a nurse in the hospital where his boy and his little wife had been taken after they were killed outright. They had been in the mortuary but the baby – twelve weeks old – had looked at Melissa and given her the most beautiful smile.

'She will never know them,' Melissa had said through her streaming tears.

'We will be her parents, darling,' he had said, being mannish, putting a comforting arm round her shoulders and realizing in that moment that his future would change irrevocably. He thought of all the years stretching ahead and for a minute – one brief minute – he had rejected utterly the thought of taking on a baby that would grow up into a girl who he would have to act as a father to. He had only had two sons and knew nothing about rearing females. But then the gentle side of him, the side that had wept when one of his soldiers had been blown to smithereens, when one of his pets had died, when poor Samba had lost his tail, took over his thoughts. And he had tickled the baby and watched her smile and had thought only of the immediate future. But now he must blunder on. Hoping that, perhaps, he would not have to undertake the dreaded deed. Praying that fate would open another path to him.

Out in the silvery moonlight pretty Isabelle, little Belle, was dancing. She was wearing a dress of white chiffon which Chris O'Hare had given her as he had dropped on his knees before her and said, 'Oh, daughter of the Dark Master. I love you eternally. Let us be together. Always.'

At these words something had triggered in Belle's mind and she looked back on recent events with a kind of growing horror. It was if she had suddenly become twins and knew what her evil side had done and she was struck with a dreadful sensation of loathing and fear.

'No,' she said. 'Go away. It's you who made me be wicked. I don't like you any more. I'm going home.'

He looked at her in that extraordinary light, his blond hair bleached white, his skin like parchment.

'Don't say that to me,' he moaned pathetically. 'I worship you. I have sought you all my life.'

Then she turned and ran, her feet seeming to float above the ground as she made her way to the only building she could see, the deserted children's orphanage that reared against the vivid sky like a vast and menacing shadow.

Daft Dickie Donkin was sitting in what had once been the dining hall of that building created by the nation's Victorian do-gooders. Tiny babies, teenaged boys, girls who wandered in a daze from place to place, had been herded by sharp-faced women in black bombazine and bonnets who had led them to this terrifying asylum where they could all be brought up together and turned into clean and decent folk who would eventually take their place in the world as a servant. The great, deserted building certainly loomed magnificently from a distance, but close to it was decaying. The ornately decorated fireplace in the drawing room was slowly disintegrating and graffiti-sprayers had been at work all over the walls with words like SMEAR, RIP, KT LUVS MJ, TITS.

The vast edifice was a huge attraction to youngsters from around and about. It was obviously the place to go to smoke weed or snort cocaine or for a quickie, many broken and narrow beds still occupying the dormitories, waiting for owners who would never return. Or even, if you dared your parents' wrath, a place to spend the night. This was not so greatly favoured as the building had a reputation for being haunted and it was said that a girl in Victorian orphanage clothes would walk weeping through the various rooms. But she was not so frightening as the shape of the boy of fourteen who had hanged himself from the rafters and dangled there to this day, for those who had the eyes to see him.

Dickie had thought the old place quiet and peaceful, blissfully unaware that small figures had darted like rats at the whispered word that he was approaching. Even the toughest kid in the neighbourhood would not dare to take on the old mad tramp, whose size and bulk alone were enough to frighten even the biggest little man. So it was appreciating the quiet and the solitude that Dickie sat in a chair, which sighed with age as his bulk descended on it. The landlady of The Barley Mow had given him a packet containing some leftover sandwiches, which he had been greatly pleased with. And now he opened the parcel to reveal an assortment of brown and white. Like a child he saved his favourite cheese and onion to the last and began by stolidly munching his way through an egg and cress on white. And then he heard a noise coming from above. It was weeping.

Dickie had heard the ghost stories surrounding the old place many times and was neither frightened nor perturbed by them. Instead he went on eating his sandwiches, wondering what was going to happen next. The white floating figure drew alongside him and turned to look at him. He saw huge black eyes with all the sorrows of the world written in them. He saw a weary, dreary little face. He smiled at it and held out his pack of sandwiches but she merely sighed and floated on her way, straight through

the dining room wall and into the room beyond. Dickie shook
his head and decided that he wasn't at all nervous of ghosts.

He snoozed for a while and then was woken abruptly by another
sound. This came from outside and was definitely of human origin.
Someone else was approaching the building. Moving carefully,
Dickie proceeded from the dining room into the great hall and
then out of what had once been a magnificent front door. Then
he stood, blinking like a cave-dweller in the sudden importuning
light of the moon. Gradually his eyes refocused and he found that
he was looking at another ghost. A little figure dressed in white,
pale blonde hair swinging round its shoulders as it turned slowly
round and round in a strange, unworldly dance of its own making.
But then his whole body shuddered with shock as he realized that
he was looking at *her*. He stood motionless, hoping that she would
not see him, for she was the demon who had lain on his chest
and stared into his eyes as he woke up but, he encouraged himself,
he had thrown her off on that occasion so was perfectly capable
of doing so again.

But then, unbelievably, a morris dancer came into view.
Blackened face, plumed top hat, tattercoat, black trousers with
bells tied on. Aware of him, the girl stopped in her tracks.

'Why have you come?'

'Looking for you, of course. You don't think I'm going away,
do you?'

'I told you to leave me alone.'

He laughed, a deep, sullen sound. 'Listen, little child of Satan.
You have nowhere to go but with me. Now that your parents
know what you have done – oh, yes, they know all right – they
will never see you again. You are hated and reviled by all those
who do not understand your presence here. Only I do and I have
sworn to the Great Master that I will defend you for the rest of
my life.'

She stared at him, her eyes growing wider so that it seemed
to Dickie they were two vivid coals burning in the middle of her
face.

'I want to see my mother. I know she'll take me back whatever
I've done.'

'Even after your recent attack on her darling pussy cat?'
answered the morris man, and laughed aloud.

She flew at him – or that's how it seemed to Dickie. She just covered the air and landed on him, all claws and vicious tearing, where he stood on the edge of the dank, decaying and empty swimming pool – a gift to the orphanage by benefactors in the twenties. He rocked at the impact and stood swaying uncertainly. His plumed hat fell backwards so that his hair turned white in the moonshine.

'You cannot kill me. I love you,' he shouted.

The girl was not human, of that Dickie was certain. For answer she spat at him and clawed his face, breaking the skin so that rivulets of blood appeared.

'Stop it, I beg you,' he roared and then, very slowly, as if the scene was being played in slow motion, the pair of them fell backwards and there was nothing, nothing but a tremendous silence.

Dickie stood, transfixed, not at all certain what he had seen. Eventually he shuffled to the edge of that cavernous opening in the ground that had once been a beautiful swimming pool, and peered downwards. They lay in the deep end amongst the piles of rotting leaves and filthy detritus that people had thrown in. They lay like lovers, not looking at all as if they had just been fighting. She, with all the evil drained from her features, appeared like a normal child, and Chris O'Hare had his blackened face close to hers as if nothing could ever tear her away from him. That they were both dead, heads completely fractured, was obvious even to the tramp.

He straightened up and decided to walk away and as he did so he said one word: 'Fate,' erupted deep from his chest, and the sound of it reverberated round the ancient walls of the crumbling orphanage.

TWENTY-TWO

Tennant had called out a huge manhunt for the child as soon as the penny had dropped as to what she really was. Yet he could still hardly comprehend it. An innocent child who tortured cats and murdered other children was almost beyond comprehension. Yet all he had to do was think of the Bulger case and his incredulity was gone in one terrible swipe. Yet for Tennant personally, though it was part of a learning curve he should long ago have come to terms with, it was only now that the full horror struck him forcibly.

Potter had taken it far more phlegmatically.

'It's all the images that we get brainwashed with, sir. Kiddies laughing and playing on TV adverts, all of 'em enjoying life with wonderful parents. Then we go back to the Victorian period when they had texts all over their houses and cards portraying curly-haired children kneeling in prayer with a band of kindly angels looking on. But it was just at that time that Constance Kent threw her four-year-old brother down the privy pan. So there's no accounting for it. Not really.'

'Do you think the child was mad?'

'Were the boys who snatched little James Bulger?'

Tennant threw his hands in the air. 'God alone knows!'

'As you say, Inspector.'

They had teams of officers and cars combing the area from Tunbridge Wells to Brighton and all outlying districts in between. And so it was that they found Hugh Wyatt, dishevelled and dirty and weeping like a broken man, sitting on the wet ground, unarmed and definitely not dangerous.

'What have we here?' said a police officer, flashing the light of a torch into his face.

'It might be a tramp,' answered another.

'No, I don't think so. I think it's one of the citizens of Lakehurst. Come on, old boy.'

They heaved him to his feet and it was then that some semblance
of normality came back to Major Wyatt.

'I've been a bloody fool,' he assured the officers. 'I've been
out looking for my granddaughter, Isabelle Wyatt, but I haven't
found her and now I'm too tired to look any more.'

One of the policemen talked rapidly into the radio on his
uniform.

'Half of Sussex police force is out looking for her, Major. May
I ask you to come along with us.'

'Can you take me home please?'

'Yes, but first of all we'd like to ask you some questions.'

'Oh, dear,' said Hugh quietly. 'I suppose you've heard all about
the recent incident.'

'No. But we'd very much like to do so.'

A solitary police car slowly drove up towards the deserted
orphanage. Another one had turned right and plunged down into
the depths of Speckled Wood.

'Spooky old place,' said one officer, staring out of the window
at the vast shape rearing up in front of him.

'It's where all the kids come for a spot of naughty, so I'm
told.'

'Well, there's no one here tonight, by the look of it.'

And as the headlights flashed across deserted windows – every
one with broken, jagged edges where bricks had been thrown
– dim and shadowy rooms, the corners of which remained pitch
black, came alive for a second.

Walking through that grim building, the only light the beam
of their torches, strained both men considerably. In fact, they
jumped violently when something scuttled in the corner and
looked at each other with decidedly grim faces.

'A rat, probably,' said one.

'Well, I'm not going to look, I'll tell you straight.'

'Nor me.'

They marched up to the dormitories and from a distant bed they
heard the sound of sobbing. They were shaking with fright, though
desperately trying not to show it, as they proceeded towards it.
But when one man put out a hand, gingerly and carefully, he
merely lifted an empty bundle of rags.

'That's enough. There's nothing living in here. Let's search the outside.'

But it was there that the greatest shock awaited them. By the light of the moon and the swing of their torches they saw the two bodies, like something from a fairy tale, the cobweb and the ogre wrapped in a firm embrace. They stood staring down, quite unable to move, thinking momentarily that the fairy moved a gossamer wing. But it was an illusion of the eerie light and, released from the spell, they phoned for backup, for forensics, for the doctor and for Inspector Tennant. Then they remained firmly in their car.

Dr Rudniski was on police duty that night and had to admit to a thrill of fear as he approached the mighty Victorian edifice and the empty swimming pool behind it. In his wild Polish imagination he could almost picture it as it must have looked when, in the 1920s, it was presented to the orphanage new. He could imagine excited little bodies, all encased in the large bathing costumes of the day, shrieking and squealing as they dived into the water, which hopefully had been heated in advance. But tonight he called for a ladder before he lowered himself into the squalor of what it had now become, all evidence of its former glory days long gone and forgotten.

The bodies had become curiously entangled as they fell and he had to push back Chris O'Hare's arms and legs from round the remains of Belle. As he did so, he heard a whisper that sounded like 'Don't', which sent a spine of fright right through him. But quickly checking, he found that the morris man had been dead an hour or two and what he thought he had heard must have been in his head.

Their skulls were badly fractured, brains and blood joining in the amalgam of muck that resided deep in what had once been a beautiful pool. At last when photographs had been taken from every conceivable angle and Dr Rudniski had been able to have a final examination before they were sent for post-mortem, the two bodies were brought up and zipped into bags before being driven away.

'What a ghastly business,' said Tennant to the doctor as he emerged, looking somewhat pale, from the depths of the pool.

'Yes, she had fought him, you know. He had scratches on his face.'

'Evil sod. Perhaps she pushed him in and then toppled accidentally herself.'

'I don't think so. He cuddled her as she was dying.'

'How strange.'

'That last moment looked rather beautiful. Their ugliness seemed washed out.'

'Don't get carried away, Doctor. He was a Satanist and she was an evil child. And I'm glad it has ended as it has. The strain of having to visit her in supervised lodging would have been too much for the major and his wife.'

'You're quite right, Inspector. It is the best ending for all concerned.'

'I think so.'

But as he turned to go Tennant could not resist one last look at the pool, on the side of which he could have sworn he momentarily saw a little girl in a white frock dancing and dancing in the moonlight.

TWENTY-THREE

Samba the cat, battered and limping slightly, nonetheless survived and after recuperating at the vet's, came to join the Wyatts in their new home, a small cottage in Virgins Lane, close to the centre of Lakehurst but fairly free of traffic so that Samba could laze by their rose-covered front door. They decided that from now on they would attend church because they had begun to believe in something. They weren't quite sure what, but anything is better than nothing. Anyway, they had called in Nick Lawrence to bless their new house and drive out all evil influences and for luck Melissa had burnt white candles in every room, including the lavatory, and was glad to see that they had all burned down in the morning.

The Victorian orphanage had fallen into the hands of a clever property developer who had changed it into a series of luxury apartments. The swimming pool he had bricked in and planted a rose garden on the site. But people had seen things there, a glimpse of a girl in a white dress. And they had wondered who she was.

So despite the unpleasantness at the Medieval May Fair the vicar was quite keen to organize another, and the villagers to join in. Miss Patsy Quinn gave a great deal of thought to becoming a vicar's wife and decided that a wedding at Christmas, with a velvet dress and carols, would be lovely. Olivia tried to plan to have enough time off to marry Dominic Tennant but couldn't find a slot in her successful life. But the triumphant wedding that September was the uniting of Sir Rufus Beaudegrave and Ekaterina in the chapel at the old castle. The whole of Lakehurst turned out to cheer them on their way and it was only Jack Boggis, who upon entering the Great House exclaimed, 'My God, things have come to a pretty pass. There's no other bugger here.'

And so saying he took his usual seat, back to the room, and with much crackling of paper, ceremoniously opened the *Daily Telegraph*.

But it was Dickie Donkin who had the greatest triumph of all, though he wasn't really aware of it and never thought about it much. The art dealer from Lewes bought the whole collection of paintings for £500 and sold them on at Christie's for several thousand each, there being a great love of that sort of painting in America. In other words, Dickie shortly became a millionaire – his bank account being managed by his agent, who was scrupulously honest – and moved on to vodka. However, he still continued to plod about, and was last seen in Arundel, sitting in the sun, stretching his limbs, which these days smell fresher, and singing in his pleasant light baritone:

> *You can hear them sigh and wish to die,*
> *You can see them wink the other eye*
> *At the man who broke the bank at Monte Carlo.*